BLISSFUL AWAKENINGS

A COURTNEY BLISS ROMANCE

PENNY MAY

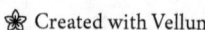

CHAPTER 1

ourtney stared out the subway train window at the couple making out on the platform. Just before the doors shut, the woman peeled herself away from her Romeo and dashed breathlessly toward the closing doors. She barely made it in time then threw herself into the seat across from Courtney. The woman caught Courtney's eyes and rolled her own while jerking her head at the man on the platform as if silently saying, "Can you believe that guy?"

Courtney wasn't sure what to do, so she demurely smiled in agreement and quickly looked away. After another boring day at the office, she was on her way to meet her boyfriend, Daniel, to have dinner at their favorite Chinese restaurant with Courtney's best friend Claire and Claire's other half Anya. This dinner was the one bright point in Courtney's calendar of events for at least the next few months. Daniel wasn't exactly Mr. Spontaneous, so they were unlikely to do anything exciting until her birthday in November.

Then Thanksgiving. Then Christmas. Then New Years.

Sometimes, Courtney felt like she was only looking forward to a few dates in the year and was just frittering away the rest of her time to get to those bright moments. She'd always thought that New York City would keep her entertained forever, yet, at some point in the last few years, it had somehow lost its shiny allure.

When she got off the train at the next stop, she looked around the platform. No Daniel. She fired off a quick text then waited until he finally responded. Apparently, rather than wait for her on the platform as agreed, he'd decided to head over to the restaurant since her train had been late.

Courtney's shoulders drooped and she trudged out of the subway station alone and down three blocks to the restaurant. She told herself that Daniel didn't need to wait for her. That she was an independent woman who didn't need her man to walk her down the street. But she also remembered when they'd first gotten together, and he'd been excited to spend more time with her. When they'd hang out for hours playing video games together or talking about movies or books. Now all he did was bury his head in his phone. And if he wasn't on that, he was playing computer games that didn't interest her.

She couldn't remember the last time they'd just sat and talked.

Or spontaneously made love.

Lately, it was wham, bam, thank you ma'am, and he went instantly to sleep or back to his video games. No snuggling afterwards or pillow talk.

When Courtney reached the restaurant, she stuffed her feelings away and put a smile on her face. No reason to bring the mood down just because she felt like her relationship was getting stale.

Inside, Courtney quickly found the three at a back booth. Daniel sipped a beer while Claire and Anya drank fun-looking cocktails. Courtney sat down next to Daniel and gave him a peck on the cheek which he barely noticed. Her smile slipped momentarily before she snapped it back in place and turned to Anya and Claire.

"Hey guys!" She said with a big smile. "Starting without me?"

When the waitress came by, Courtney ordered the same blue cocktail as Anya and found herself lost in conversation. Daniel occasionally pitched in a comment here and there, but he only fully put down his phone when the food came. The ladies smoothly incorporated him into the conversation since they were used to his lack of attention, and the conversation continued on until Daniel finished eating and slowly returned to his phone.

Courtney saw that Claire was about to make a comment about Daniel's behavior, so she cut her friend off with something she knew Claire would find interesting.

"Oh! Did you hear about the contest to get into Pleasure Temple?" She asked and took a sip of her second drink. She'd switched it up this time and ordered the pink drink that Claire had started with. It was a little sweet for her taste, but now she was stuck with it.

"Yes!" Claire said, easily taking the bait. "I can't believe two people are going to be lucky enough to get picked to go there for *free*!"

The excitement pulled Daniel from his phone. "What contest?"

Claire rolled her eyes. "Only one of the most talked about contests *ever*. Seriously, how are you on that thing all the time but somehow manage to miss the news?"

This time it was Anya who derailed a potential argument between Daniel and Claire. Such blows ups had happened in the past, and both Courtney and Anya were keen to avoid that kind of drama again. It had taken almost a year for the two to be willing to sit in the same room again, let alone talk.

"It's a contest that anyone can enter, and they randomly draw a man and a woman to be selected to live in Pleasure Temple for three months. But it ends tonight at midnight."

"Three months? Seriously?" Daniel sounded more than interested. "And they don't have to pay for it?"

Courtney shook her head. "Nope. Completely free. They even fly the lucky winners out to Vegas to get to the Temple."

Pleasure Temple had been on the lips of almost every talk show host for the past three years since billionaire owner Bo Ryans had built the monstrous high rise in the middle of the Las Vegas strip. It had been a big mystery until it was topped with a gold pyramid and the words "Pleasure Temple" in giant letters across all four sides.

Ryans had built his fortune on the illicit and well-tele-vised Fantasy Island, which was literally a small island where people could indulge in their wildest fantasies. Initially patronized by the uber-rich and famous, it eventually drew social media influencers and the "sorta-rich" who drove out the old money. Well, that and Bo turned half the island into a porn/reality TV channel. He raked in millions but only at the cost of driving away his most lucrative customers.

Word was that Ryans created Pleasure Temple to specifically meet his original clients' demands. Unlike Fantasy Island, you needed more than money to get into Pleasure Temple. You needed an invitation. And lots of money, of course.

"Can you imagine getting picked to go somewhere like that?" Courtney asked.

"It would be something, that's for sure." Claire said.

"I mean, you'd have to enter to win though. And you'd never enter something like that, would you?" Daniel asked Courtney, glancing back up from his phone again. "Plus, whoever wins would be gone for three months. No job is gonna wait that long for them."

Claire leaned toward Daniel, putting Courtney's nerves on edge. She really didn't want the evening to end on a sour note. "Maybe whoever wins won't need a job because they'll meet some ba-zillionaire who sweeps them off their feet and they live happily ever after."

"Sure, Claire." Daniel said in his I'm-about-to-pick-a-fight tone. "I'm sure that's exactly what will happen to whoever wins. Some billionaire is gonna choose some mousy, rando girl to be his wife instead of the super-hot models they've probably got over there." He suddenly turned to Courtney like she'd said something. "Go ahead and enter the contest, Babe. It's not like there's any chance you'll win."

Occasionally wanting to punch your long-term boyfriend in the face was probably not the healthiest feeling. It was like the tenth time that day she'd wondered why she stuck with him for so long. Then she'd remind herself that it was unlikely someone else would want a woman in her late twenties, who wasn't exactly on the thin side, had no real career prospects, and got excited by the idea of a great book and bubble bath.

"I hadn't planned on entering," Courtney murmured. She couldn't keep the hurt tone from her voice as she fought back the urge to cry.

"She doesn't have to enter the contest," Claire said. "I've already done it for her."

"What?" Courtney and Anya said in unison, staring at Claire.

"Oh yeah? What do you think Courtney's odds of winning are?" Daniel pressed, completely ignoring his phone now. "One in one billion? Maybe more? Because I bet that's how many people are going to enter that contest." He suddenly sat back with a triumphant smile like he'd won their argument. "Besides, if Courtney won, she'd have to leave me because I wouldn't put up with someone who whores around at Pleasure Temple. And you love me, right Babe?"

Courtney wanted nothing more than to crawl into a hole in the ground. She was embarrassed that Anya and Claire were witnessing this. There was a split second where she honestly considered leaping up and telling Daniel to shove it. She could leave Daniel. Maybe stay with Claire and Anya for a few days until she found a place of her own. Maybe she'd even move out of this gloomy city…

And then the feeling passed, and she was stuck staring at Daniel. She'd have to go home with this guy. All her stuff was there. Her cat. Her life.

"Sure, Daniel," she said. Deflated, she threw back the rest of her drink.

Dinner ended shortly after that when the conversation couldn't get back on track. Before they left, Claire hugged Courtney and confessed, "I didn't really enter you into that contest."

"That's okay. I didn't think you had. You would have told me first or sent a screenshot of the entry or something."

Claire laughed. "You're right. That does sound more like me."

The two couples went their separate ways, and though Courtney walked home with Daniel, she felt as if she was walking home alone.

* * *

THE MAN in the tailor-fitted jeans and authentic Queen concert t-shirt watched the couples leave the restaurant. As he did, he wrote down the woman's name on a napkin and tucked it in his jeans pocket. He could have looked her up right then on his phone to find out more about the woman who'd caught his eye, but he didn't. It wouldn't have been romantic. And he was a sucker for romance.

Instead, he watched her walk away, secretly willing her to enter his contest.

* * *

MOSTLY DRUNK, Courtney watched Daniel playing his computer game with his friends online. She considered trying to pry him away from it and into the bedroom, but honestly? Even drunk, she was in no mood to deal with him.

She was, however, feeling a bit rebellious.

Which was why, tucked into bed a few minutes later, she pulled up the Pleasure Temple website and entered herself into the contest. It was a small thing, but it felt weirdly freeing to hit the submit button.

Maybe tomorrow she'd take another step and start making concrete plans to leave Daniel. After all, wouldn't it be better to be alone than to be with someone who made her so miserable all the time?

With her cat curled up on the pillow behind her head, Courtney fell asleep wondering what it would be like living in Pleasure Temple.

* * *

"COURTNEY, is there a *reason* that my coffee is cold *again?*" Michelle asked, her one eyebrow raised in that way that made Courtney wonder if she'd specifically practiced in front of a mirror to get it right.

It's Thursday, Courtney sternly reminded herself. *All you have to do is get through today and tomorrow.*

She put on an apologetic smile and said, "I'm so sorry, Michelle. Let me get that warmed up for you."

Michelle ignored Courtney's outstretched hand and instead dropped the coffee in the trash can beside Courtney's desk. Coffee splashed out of the opening in the lid and spattered the floor and the side of Courtney's desk.

"Don't bother. You know it's not the same heated up. Get me a new one and get it right this time."

Somehow, Courtney managed to keep a smile on her face as she said, "Sure thing." She gathered her purse, secretly happy that she was escaping from the office even if it meant Michelle was pissed at her. Again.

"And Courtney?"

Courtney stopped, feeling caught like an escaping prisoner in the spotlight. She turned, careful to keep the smile on. "Yes?"

As the Executive Assistant to the CEO, Michelle far outranked Courtney. And she constantly took advantage of this. In fact, Courtney was pretty sure it was Michelle's goal in life to make her three assistants' lives a living hell.

Her favorite pastime was singling out lower-level employees and occasionally having her assistants leave one of those cardboard filing boxes on their desk to make them think they were being fired. If the employee reacted like they'd been fired, Michelle would tell them it was a joke and let them stay. If the employee reacted instead by laughing at the box like it was a joke, Michelle would usually fire them.

Courtney braced herself for whatever was going to come out of her boss's mouth.

Michelle pointed at the coffee mess around the trash can. "Clean this up when you get back. We can't have the office looking like a pigsty because you can't clean up after yourself."

As much as the crappy treatment irked Courtney, it

honestly ranked pretty low compared to the many times she'd been outright screamed at just for doing her job. She avoided the other assistants' eyes and focused on keeping a high-wattage smile.

"Sure thing, Michelle." She knew the chipper tone irked Michelle, so she laid it on thick as she added, "Text me if you think of anything else you need while I'm out."

She caught a few people staring as she left the office. When she got off the elevator, the people waiting outside to get on, immediately stopped their rapid conversation at the sight of her. Weird. Then again, maybe she was just being paranoid.

Once outside and free from watchful eyes, she pulled out her phone. She hadn't checked it since she'd gotten to the office this morning. Michelle had a no phones at work policy. Of course, if Courtney was out running errands for Michelle, then it was, "Why don't you answer your cell, Courtney?"

Courtney sighed. She could never win with Michelle.

Panic slipped through her mind as she looked at her phone. Five missed calls, four voicemails, and thirty-six text messages. Had something happened? One of the voicemails was from her mom so she listened to that one first.

"Courtney, hun, what's going on? My friends tell me you won some sort of pornography deal? Call me when you get the chance."

"What?" Courtney said out loud. She'd forgotten all about entering the stupid Pleasure Temple contest, and for some reason it didn't click with her mother's voicemail. Only when she listened to Claire's voicemail (skipping over two from Daniel) did she realize what had happened.

"Courtney, I *swear* I didn't enter you into that contest! Did you enter yourself? Holy shit! I can't believe you won. This is so exciting! Daniel is gonna shit a brick when he hears!"

Oh shit, Was Courtney's first thought. Not excitement. Not elation at having won something so huge. No. Her thoughts were, *Oh shit. Daniel is going to be pissed.*

She went to one of his voicemails and noted he'd called at 8:05. Five minutes after she'd started work. She hit play.

"Courtney…is this some kind of joke? *Tell* me you didn't enter that contest. I just… How could you do that? Call me back. We need to talk."

He'd hung up, then called back an hour later and left another voicemail. This one was more frantic and full of anger. "Why would you do that? How could you do this to me? Do you know what they're saying about me at work? Why aren't you calling me back? You can't go to that place. I'm telling you right now. If you go, we're done. Through. Call me back."

When the voicemail ended, Courtney had tears in her eyes. She felt panicky and guilty. Okay, yes, she'd entered the contest, but she honestly hadn't ever expected to win! How could he think she'd ever actually go to a place like that? She stared at her phone for a second before replaying the message.

This time around, Courtney realized he'd given her an ultimatum. She took a big gulp of air and tried not to cry right there in the street, her feelings at war with each other. Part of her still felt guilty for entering the contest, but a bigger part of her was indignant. Who was *he* to tell her what to do? And who cared what his work friends thought about him?

I mean, sure, it would definitely put a kink in their relationship if she went. After all, she wouldn't want him going and sleeping with other women, but—

Her phone rang while she was staring at it, and in her startled response, she automatically hit the green answer button. It was the same number that she'd already had one missed call from but no voicemail.

Before she could end the call, a man's voice said, "Hello? Courtney? Courtney Bliss?

She pressed the phone to her ear and tried to keep her voice from wavering, "Hi, yeah. This...this is Courtney."

"Oh good. Courtney, it's so good to speak with you. I wanted to be the first person to congratulate you on winning the Pleasure Temple contest." The man's voice was deep, warm, and self-assured. This was someone who was used to having people listen to him. "But I'm guessing that I wasn't the first to inform you, huh?" There was a note of humor in his tone that made Courtney feel like they were sharing a joke.

"Oh. Ah, thanks. No, you're not the first." She wasn't sure what else to say, so she asked, "Uh, who is this again?"

"My apologies. I should have introduced myself. I'm Bo Ryans. I own Pleasure Temple."

Courtney's mouth dropped open, and her knees almost gave out. Was she seriously speaking with Bo Ryans? She covered her mouth with her hand and stared at the phone.

Was this seriously happening?

"Courtney? Are you still there?" His voice came out tinny until she put the phone back to her ear. As if reading her mind, he added, "I promise it's really me. Please don't hang up. I hate when people hang up. I then have to call them back, and then...it's just awkward and embarrassing all around." He was silent for a second. "Courtney?"

Courtney quickly pulled her hand away from her mouth. "I'm still here," she hastily reassured him. "Um, are you sure it's me? I mean," she quickly clarified, "are you sure I really won the contest?"

"Well," she could hear the gentle smile in his voice and

picture him clear as day as he said in that charming Bo Ryans way of his, "your name *is* Courtney Eleanor Bliss, correct?"

"Y-yes."

"Then congratulations! You've won ten thousand dollars and an all-expense paid trip for a three month stay at Pleasure Temple. One of my assistants will be in touch with you shortly to set everything up. I hope to meet you in person soon, Courtney."

Before he could hang up, Courtney said, "Wait! Um, I'm not sure…I'm not sure I can go. I have a cat you see and—"

"That's not a problem, Courtney," he smoothly interrupted before she could make any kind of mention of having a job or a boyfriend. "Plenty of our guests bring animals. You'll have your own luxurious room for you and your cat. You can even have the balcony fenced in so your little kitty— what's his name?"

"Dot."

"So Dot can play outside. Trust me, Courtney. This trip is going to change your life." When she didn't respond, he said, "I'll see you soon," and hung up, leaving Courtney to stare at her phone again.

The reality of what was happening started to sink in as she scrolled through text messages. Most were from Daniel, urging her to call him back. A couple from Claire were filled with just exclamation marks, the words "10K" and "Vegas Baby!"

Some of the texts were from work colleagues.

Shit. No wonder people were staring at me, she thought and turned red with embarrassment. *Oh man. What is Michelle going to think of this?* She wondered and hurried to the coffee shop like she was supposed to be doing instead of taking personal calls during her work errand.

Not that it will make a difference since no matter how quick I am, Michelle will say I took too long anyways, Courtney thought after ordering and waiting for the coffee. She didn't bother to get one for herself since that would only add fuel to the flames of Michelle's wrath.

Before she knew it, Courtney was speed-walking back to the office, carefully transporting a piping hot triple, venti, half sweet, non-fat, caramel macchiato. She'd asked for it to be hotter than normal just so it would be a Michelle-approved temperature when she handed it to her boss.

Her mind raced as she hurried back to work.

What should I do about the contest? Should I go? Can I take the money and not go? Would I be giving up something amazing if I didn't go? What would someone like me do in a place like that? I'd be so out of place.

And of course, *What do I do about Daniel?*

Her phone rang just before she opened the door to re-enter the building. She glanced down at the read-out. It was Daniel.

Crap.

She weighed whether or not to answer and finally decided that not answering would only make Daniel angrier. She'd rather deal with an annoyed Michelle for the day than a pissed-off Daniel forever. Stepping away from the door so as not to be overheard by other employees entering the building, she took a deep breath and hit the answer button. Before she could even say hello, Daniel was reaming her out.

"Finally! Finally, she picks up her phone. What, you're too good to talk to me now?"

"Chill, Daniel. I was at *work*. You know that Michelle doesn't let me check my phone while I'm there. I just went out to get her another coffee, and I saw all your calls and texts." It was mostly true.

"Oh, sure. So, you *didn't know* that you'd won until just now? Come off it, Courtney. You weren't answering because you didn't want to tell me." There was a beat of silence in which Courtney got the feeling that they had an audience of Daniel's co-workers listening to them. Then he pushed forward with, "How could you enter that contest after I told you not to?"

Courtney's mouth dropped open and she tried to stay coherent as she answered. "First off, you didn't tell me not to do anything. In fact, you said 'go ahead and enter.' So, I did. Secondly," she said, annoyed that she was starting to cry in anger, "you don't get to tell me what to do. You're my boyfriend. Not my father."

"Oh, so, what? Are you just going to go off to Pleasure Temple all by yourself? Then what? Because I'm telling you right now, Courtney, I won't be here when you get back. Understand?"

"You know what, Daniel? I'm not coming back. And," she belatedly added, "you're a real asshole. We're done."

In triumph, she hit the end button and cut off whatever he'd been about to say.

For about three seconds, she felt...free.

Then reality set in.

Had she really just broken up with her boyfriend and called him an asshole?

Shit.

If she and Daniel weren't dating, she'd have to move out. Like, today. But where would she go?

A text from Claire popped up: Well???? Are you going? The suspense is killing meeeee!!

Courtney texted back: I broke up with Daniel. I'm going.

Claire: Yeeeeaaaaassssssss!

Courtney: Um...can I stay at your place tonight?

Claire: Of course!

She had to take a moment to compose herself after that. It was almost harder to reign in her anger at Daniel than any sense of grief she felt at such an abrupt end to the longest romantic relationship she'd ever had.

Who does he think he is? She kept thinking as she rode the elevator up to her office. With a shake of her head, she fought to drop her work-smile back in place as the elevator doors opened and she made her way past the receptionist to Michelle's office.

She was so wrapped up in her anger that she almost didn't notice the stares and the hushed silence that fell over her co-workers as they saw her.

Finish your errand and then deal with it, she told herself.

And then she noticed the cardboard box sitting on her desk. She came to a complete halt, staring at the box. Was she seriously about to be fired on the same day she'd just broken up with her boyfriend? She'd be homeless *and* jobless if that were the case.

Michelle's demanding voice snapped Courtney back to reality.

"Are you going to stand there staring at your desk and let my coffee get cold *again?*"

Courtney turned to the woman and pointed to the box. "There's a box on my desk."

She realized how stupid she sounded, but, like, *what the hell?*

"Why yes. Yes, there is." Michelle crossed her arms over her chest. Something that Courtney had found was the precursor to some of Michelle's more vicious actions. "Why do you suppose that is?"

Courtney opened her mouth, then closed it again. She honestly had no idea. She hadn't been gone *that* long getting Michelle's coffee. She quickly went over her past week of work. Had she forgotten an important project? Missed some significant task?

Wait, is she pulling the whole fired-not-fired joke? Courtney wondered. In that case, if she laughed it off, she'd certainly be fired.

Suddenly, all her anger at Daniel crashed together with the anger from the past three years of working for his horrible woman that she'd been bottling up. If she hadn't still been holding Michelle's damn coffee, she would have crossed her arms as well. Instead, she stood a little straighter and squared off with the other woman.

"It *looks* like you're firing me, though I'm not sure what I've done to deserve it."

Michelle laughed. "You're kidding, right?" When Courtney only stared back, Michelle shook her head. "Everyone knows you won that *contest*, Courtney." The disgusted emphasis Michelle put on the word "contest" made it sound like she's just discovered someone had taken a giant shit on her desk. "You can't hide something like that from me."

"I wasn't trying to *hide* anything." Courtney couldn't keep the annoyance out of her voice. Not that it mattered at this point. She was pretty sure from Michelle's tone that she was actually getting canned here. "I only just found out myself while getting your coffee."

As if she suddenly remembered the errand she'd sent Courtney on, Michelle stuck out her hand. "I'll take that. Then you can pack up your stuff and get out. This is not the kind of work environment for someone who stays in a house of sin."

She could feel herself almost shaking in rage. All this time spent groveling for this woman and this was the thing she was getting fired for?

There was a split second in which Courtney seriously considered throwing the cup of coffee at this horrible woman. She would more than deserve it. In fact, the office might give Courtney a standing ovation…then she realized that throwing the coffee could be considered assault, and Michelle was just the kind of person who would press charges for something like that.

Instead, Courtney laughed in her boss's face. "A house of sin? Really?" She shook her head. "The only people who say stuff like that are people who don't know what good sex actually *is*." Okay, not that Courtney thought *she* knew what good sex was, but it felt like the best comeback in that moment.

"You know what?" Courtney continued and rather than hand her boss the coffee, she popped the lid off and dropped the whole damn thing into her desk's trash can. The resulting splash almost (but unfortunately not quite) hit Michelle.

"I quit."

Without a backward glance, Courtney left the office for the last time.

It was strangely gratifying to finally get the chance to tell off her horrible boss. She was so glad she would never have to go back there again, too. Since Michelle had always prohibited any personal items in the office, it wasn't like she even had anything to pack up to take with her. She already had her purse in hand, so once she left, she was free and clear.

Her elation at quitting carried her all the way to the train station where, the moment she stepped on the train, she remembered that now she'd have to go home and pack all her belongings.

Today was apparently going to be a day of endings.

On the way home, she called her mom back and had a super awkward conversation to explain that going to Pleasure Temple was an opportunity to get out of New York. Her mom had been unsure about the whole thing until Courtney told her she'd broken up with Daniel. Then her mom flipped her whole attitude upside down and was all for Courtney going to the Temple.

"You're still so young, hun. Go. Have fun. Meet some other men. Then after three months, you can do something new. Think of it like a three-month break to figure things out."

Courtney couldn't believe her mom had hated Daniel enough to be excited about her only daughter going to what conservatives labeled a "brothel in the desert."

By the time she got halfway home, her mom had convinced her to at least accept the cash prize so that she could use it toward securing a new apartment by herself. Though her mom had tried really hard to talk Courtney into moving in with her for a short time, Courtney didn't feel like that would be the right move right now. Not only because she didn't want to have to move back in with her mom in her twenties, but because she didn't want to go from depending on Daniel to depending on her mom.

Maybe it was time to be alone for a little bit.

Then again, how alone would she be in a luxury vacation resort that specifically catered to pleasuring guests?

She shook the thought from her mind and focused on the next steps.

Bo Ryans had said she'd be hearing from his assistant. She'd just have to wait for them to call. In the meantime, she could go home and pack a suitcase to stay at Claire's tonight. Should she bring Dot? Or maybe she should leave her cat at the apartment overnight and go back tomorrow to collect Dot and her other stuff?

The rest of her ride home was filled with a mix of excitement and fear of the unknown. Her thoughts swirled back to her conversation with Daniel. She still couldn't quite believe she'd stood up to him. Maybe this really was the push she'd needed to move on like her mom had said.

A tiny part of her kept suggesting she call him back and beg for his forgiveness. That she was rocking the boat and should just forget the whole contest thing.

But honestly, how often did an opportunity like this come up?

No.

She had to do it. She needed a change in her life, and Pleasure Temple was going to be that change.

CHAPTER 2

 hen Courtney got back to her apartment, the reality of her choice came crashing down on her. How was she supposed to pack up all her stuff? And if she did, what would she even do with it? She couldn't just leave it at Claire and Anya's place. Maybe she could just use some of her contest winnings to rent a storage unit? But then she'd still have to rent a truck to haul her stuff over there. Plus, there was the actual moving stuff part. Ugh. It all seemed too much.

Should she just call Daniel back and apologize?

She'd felt so excited and ready for change on her way home. It had been just like she'd seen in so many movies where the main character leapt into something new and changed their life for the better…

Hollywood never mentioned the part where you second-guess yourself and wonder if maybe you're making a huge mistake.

Just as Courtney had this thought, the front door buzzer went off. She moved Dot off her lap, where the cat had been trying to comfort her, and hit the speaker button. "Yes?"

"Is this Courtney Bliss"

"Yes…?"

"Great! I'm so glad I caught you. I'm Olivia Watson. I believe Bo mentioned that I'd be coming by?"

"Um, he mentioned someone would be contacting me." She hesitated, not wanting to sound ungrateful. "I didn't realize you'd be coming here in person. That was fast."

Olivia sighed. "Sometimes Mr. Ryans likes to work so quickly that he forgets the details." She paused, then added, "Actually, between you and me, I think he's afraid you'll change your mind. Do you mind if I come up so we can make some arrangements?"

Why would Bo Ryans care if she didn't go to Pleasure Temple? Maybe it was a public relations thing. Can't have the big contest winner snubbing the prize. Courtney decided that must be it, then realized Olivia was waiting for a response.

"Oh, yes. I'm sorry. Of course." Courtney hit the button to open the downstairs door. Seconds later, she answered her front door to Bo's assistant. Olivia was a tall black woman who gave an impression of authority with a flair for fun. She wore a bright red leather jacket over a white blouse, navy blue slacks, and low-heeled red shoes. Her outfit screamed professional and badass at the same time.

She entered the apartment with a smile. "Hi Courtney, it's so nice to meet you. Congratulations on winning the contest!"

"Thanks!" Courtney automatically shifted her tone to match Olivia's enthusiasm. She was determined to be happy about this, damn it. "Please, come in." She stepped back and waved Olivia into the apartment, then was immediately aware of how unkempt the space was.

Though Courtney tried to keep the place clean, sometimes she felt like she was picking up after a toddler who couldn't be bothered to clean up his own mess. She managed most of the household chores like dishes and laundry, but she'd been working on getting Daniel to at least take the damn dishes into the kitchen to deposit them in the sink. As a result, he had two dirty glasses and three coffee mugs stacked around his computer desk. That, added to the many empty energy drink cans laying around his space, made their apartment appear messier than Courtney had realized.

The rest of the place was actually pretty clean, but since Daniel's computer space was one of the first things guests saw when anyone entered the apartment, Courtney was a bit embarrassed by it.

"Sorry, I should have cleaned up. Mr. Ryans just said someone would be in touch. I guess I didn't realize you'd be coming in person," Courtney repeated to hide her embarrassment.

"Ah, Bo. Like I said, he's not great with the details." Olivia's grin was a silent invitation not to feel embarrassed and caused Courtney to smile back. "Actually, I tried to connect with you at your place of work, but they said you didn't work there anymore?"

"Actually, they fired me this morning when they found out I'd won the contest." Though she'd decided that getting a new job and breaking up with Daniel was going to be *a good thing, damn it*, Courtney had never been fired from a job before and saying it out loud made her throat constrict with emotion.

"I see," Olivia's smile disappeared. "You know, that could be a bit of a PR nightmare for them if, let's say, the press was to find out that they'd fired you for something happening in your personal life." She cocked her head to the side just enough to let Courtney know that her musing was an option and Courtney merely had to say the word.

It only solidified Courtney's impression that Olivia was not a woman to trifle with.

"Oh, that's okay. I mean, it's not like I liked the job or anything. My boss was such a..." Courtney trailed off trying to find a polite way to describe Michelle.

"Bitch?" Olivia helpfully supplied. "I got that impression when I spoke with her a little bit ago. How long did you work there?"

"Three years."

"Jesus. You should be sainted for putting up with her shit for that long."

Courtney smiled and tried not to get emotional about a complete stranger making her feel a little more understood. Working for Michelle really had been a shitty three years. Why had she put up with it for so long? Oh, yeah. Because she lived in New York and needed the money just to make rent, let alone have a life.

Olivia carefully watched Courtney, then unslung a designer purse from her shoulder. "Is there somewhere we can sit to go over some paperwork? It's nothing crazy. Just some formalities in regard to winning the contest."

"Oh, sure." Courtney led them to the kitchen table which was thankfully clear of the junk mail normally piled there. They both sat, and Olivia pulled a stack of documents from her purse and set it in front of Courtney. It definitely looked like more than just a few formalities.

Seeing Courtney's expression, Olivia quickly reassured her. "I know. It looks overwhelming, right? But I promise it's not that bad. It's a fairly basic contest agreement that lays out your winnings." She started flipping through the stack of papers and laying each sheet in front of Courtney as she did. "This one says you've won ten thousand dollars—and if I were you, I'd set some of that aside for the taxes you'll get hit with. Not that I'm giving you financial advice, mind you." She smiled, then continued on, setting another paper in front of Courtney. "This one is a nondisclosure agreement that says you agree not to tell anyone the identities of the other guests at the Temple." She tapped the paper, and Courtney noticed that her fingernails were painted the same shade as her jacket and shoes. "This is a really big deal. You're likely to rub elbows with some of the one-percenters."

"One-percenters?" Courtney interrupted.

"They're the richest people in the world. Usually the most powerful, too. They've also signed all the same paperwork here. Except the contest winnings agreement of course. But this paper," she tapped the nondisclosure agreement again, "this one also protects you. It means people aren't allowed to talk about their experiences at the Temple or who those experiences were with except for in the vaguest of ways."

Courtney gave Olivia a look, so the other woman explained, "When people talk about going to the Temple, they all sound the same right? 'Oh, it was so amazing. It was ecstasy. I could live out my deepest fantasy, blah, blah, blah.'" She shook her head. "It's all vague nonsense because they signed this form. What you do in the Temple stays in the Temple."

Courtney started to nod, then stopped, "Except, everyone already knows I'm going there, right? Because of the contest?"

"True," Olivia admitted, "but this paper keeps anyone there from talking about what they might see you doing. Or from talking about what happens if you decide to spend an evening with them. Honestly? You could go to the Temple and never touch or talk to another living being if you wanted to. No one would ever know." She shrugged. "What you do while you're there is up to you."

That sounded a lot more appealing to Courtney. She wasn't a total prude, but she wasn't sure she was ready to dive into the deep end of some of the crazier things she'd seen or heard about at Fantasy Island. It seemed like things would only be kinkier at Pleasure Temple since no one could talk about it.

Olivia walked Courtney through some other documents: an agreement to get tested for STD's, an agreement to remain on some form of birth control during her stay, and then some pretty standard rental agreements about how she'd be responsible if she damaged any property in the room she'd have at the Temple.

When Olivia finished explaining the stack of paperwork, she put a pen on top of the stack.

"Okay, if you're in, and you'd like a free, three-month stay in one of the ritziest, most pleasurable places in the world, go to it."

Courtney looked at Olivia for a second. She'd only just met her, but she liked Olivia's straightforward personality. Sure, maybe Olivia was just really good at schmoozing people, but Courtney didn't think that was the case.

Which is why, before signing anything, she asked, "If you were me, seriously, would you do this? Would you drop everything and disappear for three months to live at the Temple?"

"In a heartbeat. I've worked for Bo for six years, first at Fantasy Island as an assistant to an assistant to an assistant—you know how it is—"

Courtney nodded. As an ex-assistant to an executive assistant, she knew exactly how it was.

"I eventually worked my way up the ranks, and now I'm one of two assistants who work directly for Bo."

"Wow, that's awesome," Courtney said. And she meant it. Working your way up the ladder to be an assistant for a billionaire CEO of several companies meant Olivia kicked ass at her job.

"I've seen everything you can imagine at both Fantasy Island and Pleasure Temple, and, truth be told, I've been gifted a weekend here and there to stay at the Temple as a vacation. Do you know what I did?"

Courtney shook her head, thinking that Olivia wouldn't possibly give her details after going through the importance of the nondisclosure agreement.

"The first weekend? I slept. I slept and read the whole damn weekend. It was amazing. Food and drinks were brought to my door. I had a balcony with an amazing view. It was one of the best, most relaxing vacations I've ever had." She leaned in conspiratorially to Courtney. "But my second weekend staying there? I had wild, amazing, mind-blowing sex. And that was pretty great, too."

Courtney tried not to look shocked. She really didn't even talk about sex with Claire, her closest friend. It just wasn't something she felt comfortable talking about. She'd been raised to keep what happened between the sheets to herself.

Olivia leaned back again. "So, if I had a chance to go for three months, all expenses paid? Absolutely." She shook her head. "Look, Courtney, this experience will be what you make of it. If you want to hang out by yourself in your room, eat popcorn all day, and watch movies? That's okay. The point of the Temple is literally pleasure. So, if that's the thing that makes you happy, then that's what you should do."

When she put it that way…

"Thanks. I think that's what I needed to hear."

With that, Courtney picked up the pen and started signing the paperwork. When she was done, Olivia pulled one more sheet of paper from her purse, and Courtney almost groaned at the sight of another document to sign. Her hand was tired from all that work!

"I saved the best for last. It wasn't mentioned in the contest, but one of the prizes is an all-inclusive makeover by some of the most exclusive stylists around. Hair, makeup, nails—the whole shebang. You'll also get a full wardrobe from a mix of different designers as part of the contest winnings."

Courtney's mouth fell open. She had barely been able to buy nice blouses for work, let alone anything designer. "Really?"

"Yes, really."

Once Courtney had signed the last document, Olivia gathered all the paperwork, tucked it back into her purse which doubled as a briefcase, and turned back to Courtney. "So, during the duration of your makeover and your three-month stay, Bo has assigned me to work as your assistant. Do you have an idea of when you'd like to actually come and stay at the Temple?"

"Oh, uh. I was actually thinking of coming sooner rather than later, if that's possible?" For some reason, Courtney felt embarrassed to be asking to go so soon after having acted insecure about going. She quickly explained, "I might have just broken up with my boyfriend." Only, instead of making things sound better, somehow that made things worse. "I mean, I have somewhere to stay tonight, but—"

Thankfully, Olivia cut her off before she could continue digging a pit of embarrassment.

"Sooner is always better when it comes to getting to the Temple. We'll need to make some appointments, but I bet we could get you out to the Temple in about a week. We might have to go with designers who are little less in demand, though, since it sort of depends on their schedule."

It was a much faster timeline than Courtney was expecting. All she could say was, "Of course."

"In the meantime," Olivia looked around just as Dot came to investigate why Courtney's visitor hadn't come to pet her yet. "Hello, kitty." She looked up, "Bo says Dot is coming with you?"

Damn. Olivia was good. Courtney hadn't told her Dot's

name, but Bo must have prepped her before she came over. Impressive. And...it gave Courtney a warm and fuzzy feeling that Bo Ryans, billionaire and multi-business owner, had bothered to remember her cat's name.

"Uh yeah," Courtney tried not to stammer. "If that's okay?"

"Oh sure. Just as long as she's not part of the fun." Courtney gave her a confused look, so Olivia explained, "There's a strict no bestiality rule at the Temple."

"Oh my god, no! I'd never do that," Courtney spluttered, face turning red in embarrassment.

"You'd be surprised what people are into. So, some quick ground rules. No bestiality, no underage sex, and all physical interactions must be by consent of both partners."

Courtney nodded. Those all sounded like pretty good rules honestly.

"I'll explain more when we get to the Temple. For now, let's plan out the next few days so we're on the same page."

From there, Olivia did just that. It was a whirlwind of planning, and though Courtney insisted she could stay at Claire's house until she left for the Temple, Olivia overruled her and set Courtney up in a posh hotel that Bo Ryans' company would pay for.

"It's the least we can do since you lost your job over winning the Temple contest," Olivia explained.

They hammered out a time to meet the next day, and then Olivia left. Before she did though, she stopped and threw a quick look around the apartment. "You know, your rooms at the Temple will be fully furnished. The only things you really need are some clothes for the next few days and any personal items you can't live without." She looked back at Courtney and after a second, finally seemed to come to a decision before saying, "I know you didn't ask for my advice, but I'm gonna give it anyways: Make it a clean break. Where you're going, you won't need any of these things. Except for Dot's kitty stuff, of course," she added as the cat wound around her legs.

"What about after the three months are up?"

Olivia smiled at her. "Things have a way of working themselves out."

She turned to leave, then stopped. "Oh my gosh, I almost forgot." She pulled a credit card from the side pocket of her bag and handed it to Courtney. "Here's your ten thousand bucks. Don't spend it all in one place. And don't forget what I said about taxes. Seriously."

She then disappeared out the door, leaving Courtney staring after her in open mouth wonder at what felt like a magic credit card in her hand.

Once she'd recovered from her shock, she turned to inspect her apartment with fresh eyes. This morning, she'd woken up and gone to work feeling like she had little to look forward to in life. Now she'd just literally been handed a bunch of money and would soon be rubbing elbows (and maybe other things) with some of the richest and hottest people in the world.

She thought maybe she should lie down for a moment, but when she looked at the time, she realized Daniel would be home in a few hours. She didn't want to be there when he got home, so she needed to make some quick decisions on what she wanted to take with her.

Room by room, she thought and stood looking in the kitchen for a moment. There were the pots and pans from college she'd gotten from her mom as hand-me-downs. None of them were family heirlooms nor were they antiques, so it would be no real loss to leave them. After a few moments of hesitation, she decided on the milk-glass vase that had been her grandmother's and her favorite mug that was a gift from Claire. On the side was a hand giving the middle finger and writing underneath that cautioned, "Come back when I've had my coffee."

Courtney had never been brave enough to take it to work.

Next up: the living room. Stacks of DVD's and books waited for her there. She felt pretty overwhelmed at first, then realized she didn't actually need to take any of that stuff with her. If she wanted to read her favorite books again, she could just download them on her phone. The same went for the movies. With that, she was able to mentally check the living room off her list.

She moved on to the bedroom. First, she pulled a small roller suitcase from the back of her closet, threw it on the bed, and opened it.

"Okay," she said to Dot who had jumped on the bed and was trying to stealthily move toward the suitcase. "Yes, you're going with me, Dot." She touched the namesake dot on the cat's head like a button as she always did, then turned back to the closet and chest of drawers before her.

After a bit of hemming and hawing, she finally chose her ten favorite tops, two pairs of jeans, her only black dress, and a skirt she adored but rarely wore along with two pairs of dress shoes. She'd just wear her more comfortable work shoes to the hotel. As an afterthought, she chucked in a pair of newer running shoes she'd barely had the chance to use. Maybe they'd have a treadmill at the Temple? She hoped to get back into running, but college track seemed like a long time ago.

She paused after throwing her everyday underwear into the suitcase. After a moment, she dug through the drawer and revealed a red, barely-there piece of lingerie that she'd bought to surprise Daniel with on his birthday.

"What the hell," she told Dot and threw it in with her

other clothes. Maybe she'd change her mind and take a little walk on the wild side while she was at the Temple.

After that, decisions were easy. Her toiletries went into the suitcase, and then she made up a bag of Dot's toys, food, treats, and her favorite fluffy blanket. It was a fight to get Dot into the cat carrier since she usually only used it for vet visits. The trick was to put the cat in backwards. Once Dot settled in the carrier after a few annoyed meows, Courtney was pretty much ready to go.

At the last minute, she cleaned out the litter box, then put the litter box itself into a garbage bag. She planned to toss it before going to the Temple since she could just pick one up somewhere there, but she'd need the litter box for however long she'd stay at the hotel.

Throughout her whirlwind of packing, Courtney had been trying to figure out how she was going to get all her stuff over to the hotel. It wasn't a lot, but it was more than she could handle by herself on the train or by bus. As she sat down, somewhat exhausted by her efforts, she realized the answer to her problem was in her pocket. She didn't have to take the subway. She could call a car service to pick her up right outside the apartment.

She pulled out the card and smiled down at it, feeling a little like Sméagol looking at his Precious. After scheduling a ride and paying with the card, she giggled. She could get used to this. Having money sure did make things a lot easier. Her spirits start to lift—

—and then the front door opened, and Daniel walked in.

CHAPTER 3

"Well? What did you do then?" Claire asked, leaning in and listening intently as she sipped on a second mojito.

They sat in the hotel bar, snacking on fancy hors d'oeuvre and sucking down cocktails. It was the first time Courtney had spent time alone with Claire in a long time. Usually either Daniel or Anya was with them. She realized that it was kind of nice just to have her friend to herself for a bit. It reminded her of what it was like when they were roommates.

"What did I do? I got the hell out of there!" Courtney said and realized she was being a little too loud when the bartender and another guest at the end of the bar glanced her way. She lowered her voice as she continued, "Daniel said he had come home early to try and make up with me," here she paused and made a face at her friend, "but what he was *really* trying to do was convince me not to go." Courtney shook her head, pissed just thinking about how Daniel had tried to make her feel bad for leaving when it had been *his* ultimatum that they break up if she went! "Honestly? I think he cares more that I won't be there to cook and clean for him anymore."

"Probably, but I'm sure he'll miss more than that when you've been gone for a while," Claire said then quickly raised a hand to shield against Courtney's raised brow. "I'm not defending him. God knows I'm the *last* person who would take up for him. I'm just speaking facts here. First, he'll miss the stuff that's visible like the cleaning and cooking thing, then he'll start to notice he's all alone with no one to talk to. Not to mention, the lack of sex thing."

Courtney rolled her eyes playfully at her friend. "Because we were having *so* much sex." It made Claire laugh as Courtney intended but it was kind of embarrassing to admit anything about her sex life, even to her best friend. She swirled the fancy straw around in her cocktail for a moment before looking up at her friend again. "I kind of hope you're right, that Daniel will miss more than me just acting like a cleaning service for him, but even if he does, I won't be going back to him. I've just been so miserable, Claire." Courtney couldn't help but look back down at her drink, too embarrassed to make eye contact with her friend as she admitted, "I just refused to see that my relationship with him had fallen apart until I had the opportunity to get out of there."

Claire nodded. "You haven't seemed very happy for at least the past year. Endings suck when it comes to relationships, and I know you loved him at some point—"

Courtney could see how hard Claire was working not to say how much she'd come to dislike Daniel in the past year and appreciated her friend all the more for not saying, "I told you so."

"—but sometimes things just dry up and end. People change." She shrugged but softened it with a smile. "I'm just glad you got the opportunity to make a clean break and start over with a trip to somewhere so amazing," Claire finished, then added, "And you know, if you decide *not* to go to Pleasure Temple, you can always stay with me and Anya until you find a place. After all," she said with a grin that ruined the moment, "it would be like having a celebrity stay with us!"

"Thanks, Claire," Courtney said while returning Claire's grin, secretly happy that her friend was so great at making their conversation less awkward. Then she groaned at Claire's reminder of being considered a celebrity.

After Courtney had checked into the hotel (and maybe had a good cry, but no one needed to know that) and gotten Dot as settled as a cat could be in a strange place, she'd called up Claire and invited her to the hotel for dinner.

The hotel that Olivia had selected was higher class than anywhere Courtney had ever stayed before, making her a little intimidated to check in. It had felt like Courtney's worst nightmare when the very fashionable clerk at the front desk initially told Courtney she didn't have anything in the system under her name.

Courtney's immediate response was to retreat, but instead she'd screwed up her courage and decided to give it a last-ditch effort. "Um, actually, I don't know if you've heard of Pleasure Temple? I, ah, won that contest and—"

"Oh my gosh!" The clerk had practically shrieked. "I read about you! But…you don't look anything like the picture in the article."

"Picture?"

The clerk had reached under the desk and pulled out her personal cell phone. After a few minutes of searching, she'd turned the phone toward Courtney.

Now, sitting with Claire after a few drinks, Courtney decided to change the subject away from Daniel to something she could laugh about (though in the moment that the front desk attendant had shown her the picture, she'd been quite mortified).

"Do you know that the news is using my old picture from college? Like, what the hell? I have, like, fifty better pictures on social media that are more current! Why use a terrible one from when I'd gained thirty pounds? Jerks."

Claire winced. "I saw that. I don't think there's much you can do about it. On the bright side, no one will realize who you are before you leave the city unless you tell them your name."

That was a good point. She should probably be grateful no one was stopping her on the street out of recognition. That would be super weird.

"I kind of can't believe you're going," Claire said looking down and swirling the ice in her drink.

"You don't think I should?"

"No, no! You should definitely go if you want to. I'm just surprised is all. You were never really that adventurous in sex from the things you've told me. I mean, remember Elizabeth?"

Courtney immediately turned red and dropped her eyes to her own whiskey sour. "So?"

"So...you thought you'd see if you were into women, and you barely made it to first base with her."

"I mean, I wasn't into it. Why would I need to go further to figure that out?"

"My point is that there's going to be a lot more options than just making out with women there. There's a whole world of sex that I don't think you've really even scratched the surface of. It doesn't mean anything bad about you that you haven't," she quickly reassured her friend, "but I just don't want you to be surprised and overwhelmed when someone shows up with a whip and chains ready to party."

Courtney winced at the thought. It wasn't really what she

was into. At least, she didn't think she'd be into that. She was a little intrigued by bondage, but what Claire said sounded more hardcore than she was ready for.

"Olivia, Bo Ryans' assistant, said that I could treat the whole thing like a luxurious vacation and never even come out of my room if I don't want to."

"Really?"

"Yup."

"But if you don't come out of your room, how will you write a tell-all book about your experience there!" Claire said only somewhat jokingly.

"Nope. No books. I had to sign a nondisclosure agreement upfront. What happens at the Temple…"

"…stays at the Temple," they finished together, followed by a gale of laughter that once again got them looks from other bar patrons.

"But seriously," Claire said when their laughter had died down, "you should really consider trying out a few things while you're there. I mean, how many times are you gonna get an opportunity like this?"

"I know, I know. I'll figure it out when I get there. I honestly don't even know what to expect."

Claire shrugged. "Well, don't do anything you don't feel comfortable with, but also life can be a lot more exciting if you step outside your comfort zone, you know? Why not test the waters and live it up a little?"

They talked for another few hours about Courtney finally quitting her job and what they would do when Courtney got back from Vegas. When Claire had to head home ("Since some of us still have to work," she'd jokingly said), Courtney retreated to her room after paying the bill over Claire's protests. She finally won that argument by telling her it was Claire who had put the idea in her head to enter the contest and had gotten her started on this path. She really felt she owed it to her friend to at least get her something. Dinner and drinks felt like a good place to start.

As she fell asleep that night surrounded by soft sheets on an amazingly cloud-like bed, Dot purring at her back, Courtney thought maybe she would pick up a fun designer purse for her friend as a more appropriate thank you.

The thought made her smile as she fell asleep.

* * *

THE NEXT DAY, Olivia took Courtney shopping for a whole new wardrobe. Courtney found it kind of exhilarating that she didn't have to drag herself to the office and put up with Michelle anymore.

She'd woken up to find herself in a strange room and panicked when she'd looked at the time and found she only had a few minutes to get ready and out the door or she'd be late for work, only to realize she didn't have a job to go to anymore. It was the first time she'd really had a day off from *everything.* Usually, her weekends had been filled with catching up on housework with the occasional book reading session thrown in between tasks.

Now she didn't even have an apartment to keep up nor a boyfriend to clean up after.

"It's just you and me, Dot," she told her cat, then lounged around her fancy hotel room for a bit, sipping coffee and petting Dot who was always more affectionate in the mornings.

As much as she wanted to just enjoy her morning off, it was a struggle not to replay the argument with Daniel in her mind. It didn't help that he'd already called her twice that morning.

In the past, Courtney's automatic response to a fight with him would have been to be angry for a day or so, then eventually apologize and make up with him even if she didn't feel she was in the wrong. Taking the blame for whatever they'd been arguing about always released the tension from their relationship and let things get back to normal.

Now, looking back on all those arguments, Courtney realized that Daniel had never once been the one to apologize or initiate any kind of truce. She had always been the one who smoothed things over. The realization made it a little easier for Courtney to continue ignoring Daniel's calls. Even if he wanted to apologize now, it was too little, too late.

By the time she met Olivia downstairs, she'd turned off her phone so she wouldn't have to be continually reminded of her breakup. Getting in the back of the chauffeured car with Olivia, she sternly told herself, *You're gonna have a fun day today, damn it,* and forced a smile on her face.

"Ready for a morning of high-end dress shopping?" Olivia asked.

"Yes!" Courtney said with enthusiasm that was maybe a little too over-the-top. If Olivia noticed her forced mood, she kept it to herself as they were whisked through Manhattan's morning traffic.

Two hours later, Courtney perched on the edge of a luxurious white leather couch clutching a mimosa in a death grip and wondering what her next mortifying chore would be during this so-called "fun" shopping experience. The moment they'd arrived at the upscale boutique, she'd been stripped down to her underwear so that practically every inch of her could be measured by the clothing designer's many assistants.

She hadn't been expecting quite so much individualized attention but tried as best she could to play it off since it seemed like the norm for getting custom designed clothes. Everything had been mostly fine until one of the assistants started making occasional remarks about Courtney's body. Of course, it had all been out of Olivia's earshot, so Courtney kept it to herself. She didn't want to cause any trouble, especially since Olivia had mentioned before that it had been difficult to get in with this designer.

Now they sat waiting in an all-white room where large, freestanding mirrors lined the walls to create a sort of runway. It reminded Courtney a little of her experience wedding dress shopping with Claire, except at least she'd had a fun time doing that.

The sound of clothing hangers being scraped across metal racks came from behind a closed door that stood directly across from the couch. Courtney tried not to flinch each time she heard the grating noise and envisioned yet another tiny dress being added to a pile that she'd have to strip down for again to try on.

Olivia occasionally glanced over to make sure Courtney was doing okay. It had become clear to Olivia about halfway through the measurement process that her new charge was out of her element and not actually having much fun. Maybe she should have warned her what to expect before their appointment.

She cleared her throat, making Courtney jump.

"Don't worry, this is the fun part." Disbelief flickered over Courtney's face before she could control her features and give Olivia that fake smile that was starting to annoy Olivia.

Courtney dropped the smile for a second, then after a quick glance around to make sure they were completely alone, confessed, "If I'd have known that I'd have to get undressed in front of everyone, I would have worn nicer underwear." Though she was a little mortified to admit it,

Courtney felt like she'd better get the lay of the land before she ran into any more surprises. "Maybe you could tell me what to expect next? I feel like I walked straight into a movie that I don't know any of the lines for."

Olivia was so used to working with Bo at this point that she hadn't considered what it might be like for someone used to buying clothes off the rack to experience a personal fitting with a known designer. It was a good thing the actual designer wasn't on site today and Courtney only had to deal with the designer's assistants.

"I'm sorry. I should have warned you what to expect."

"No, no," Courtney quickly held up her free hand. "It's not your fault. This is just all new to me." She looked around again to make sure the assistants hadn't returned yet then lowered her voice a little just in case. "So, what's next? Will I be trying things on now?"

Hearing the real apprehension in Courtney's voice, Olivia quickly squashed the smile that tugged at the corners of her mouth. "Next we'll just sit back, have our drinks refilled as needed, and watch some in-house models show you dress options from the designer."

Courtney blew out a sigh of relief. "Good. I didn't think I'd be able to fit into anything they brought out anyways after some of their comments earlier."

"What?"

"Oh, it's nothing. I mean, I'm sure they're used to skinnier women coming in here and not people like...me." Courtney gestured to her body with her mimosa. She'd never been a skinny girl but was mostly accepting of her body until she got those not-so-subtle reminders from people like the assistant today. For some reason, the remark that had stuck with her today was when the assistant told her Courtney might want to look into shape wear if she wanted to look halfway decent in their clothing line.

"What?" Olivia heard herself say again. She couldn't help it. None of her clients had ever been disrespected like that.

"It's okay," Courtney quickly said, "especially if I don't have to try anything on..." she trailed off as she watched Olivia. She could almost feel the waves of anger coming from the other woman.

"It is *not* okay. This is supposed to be a *fun* experience for you. Not a day of being body shamed." Olivia set her mimosa flute down on a side table and patted Courtney's leg before saying in a polite voice that barely masked a promise of violence, "I'll be right back."

Courtney watched with a mixture of awe and dread at causing an issue as Olivia disappeared into a back room. The sound of hangers was quickly replaced by a low murmur of voices that Courtney couldn't quite make out. Then the murmurs abruptly broke off and Olivia returned with a smile that made Courtney thankful to have the woman on her side.

Taking up her drink once again, Olivia sat and nonchalantly explained, "So, here's what to expect: They're going to show you only their top dresses. You're going to say whether you want the dress or not and they will take that dress and create a version in your actual size." She leaned forward a little and lowered her voice. "Only say yes to something you really, really like. You are under no obligation to take *anything* from them." Olivia lifted a brow, waiting for confirmation that Courtney understood. At Courtney's nod, she continued, "The only reason we're even still sitting here instead of leaving is because I don't want you to have to go through the process of being measured all over again. *I* recommend picking only a few dresses from here today. Then I'll get you scheduled to meet with a different, less well-known but more body-positive designer for later this week."

Courtney simply nodded again, unsure how else to respond.

And then the door to the backroom suddenly opened and her own private fashion show started.

The first dress was quite the showstopper with shiny gold material that hugged the model's breasts and hips before billowing out and trailing behind the woman as she made her way down the runway toward the couch. She paused in front of the couch to strike a subtle pose, then turned first one way, then the other before making her way back down the runway.

"Is that...does that dress have a cape?" Courtney whispered to Olivia.

"It does," said a woman who had suddenly appeared on Courtney's left. "They're all the rage right now, you know." The woman extended her hand to Courtney. "I'm Elouise Marion, by the way. The designer."

Courtney shook the woman's hand all the while wondering how she could possibly turn down dresses when the designer would be *standing right there!*

"So lovely to meet you in person," Olivia said and shook Elouise's hand after Courtney. Her tight smile indicated she wasn't too sure that was true.

"You must be Olivia Watson, Bo Ryans' personal assistant. So nice to meet you. I'm so pleased that you've chosen my designs to be a part of your contest." She looked back at Courtney. "It will be such an honor to have you showcase my dresses at Pleasure Temple."

Courtney wasn't sure what to say so she gave a polite smile which quickly became strained when Olivia responded, "Only a few of your dresses, unfortunately, as we're given to understand that your designs are only for women with a perfect model's figure."

Oh snap, Courtney thought, then was so thankful that

Olivia had made it clear they would only be selecting a few dresses as the next model walked down the runway in the ugliest dress Courtney had ever seen. It was lime green with poofy chiffon shoulders and a high collar that buttoned tightly around the model's neck then fell straight down to the floor with practically no shape to it.

Elouise seemed unaffected by Olivia's comment.

"Ah yes, this is my *favorite* dress of the season," the designer practically purred. "You would certainly stand out from a crowd in this and be the belle of the ball."

Courtney had to fight to keep a look of revulsion off her face and only barely managed to keep her expression in check, but not before Olivia saw it peek through.

"It's certainly eye-catching," Olivia's said dryly, "but we're looking for dresses that are a little more...sophisticated. We want Courtney to be ready for a lavish dinner party or an evening at the opera."

The designer opened her mouth to respond then thought better of it and changed whatever she was about to say. "Of course. Just one moment while I change the lineup to better fit your needs."

Olivia inclined her head, and the designer disappeared— which was fortunate because the moment Courtney looked over at her, Olivia could barely suppress her grin.

"Did you *see* that dress? You're not going to the Copacabana!" She whispered to Courtney.

Of course, this caused Courtney to lose her neutral veneer and chortle, "Oh my gosh! I'm so glad I wasn't the only one who thought so! I would look like the Jolly Green Giant in that thing!" She fought to keep her voice down as they laughed.

"Or a poofy Grinch!" Olivia barely managed to gasp between giggles.

By the time the designer returned, they'd finally gotten

themselves back under control. Courtney was actually thankful for the terrible dress as it let her reign in her nervousness and release some tension. The rest of her high-end shopping experience went much better after that. She actually ended up buying four dresses from Elouise despite the ugly comment from the assistant.

Finally, back in the car and on their way to another appointment, Olivia asked, "I thought we'd agreed on less dresses from her?"

With a shrug, Courtney explained, "I really liked those dresses. Plus, it would have felt like I was letting that assistant win if I chose not to wear her designer's clothes, you know? Like, maybe it will do some good if someone my size is wearing her designs."

"'Someone your size' is a normal, healthy woman," Olivia said firmly and gave Courtney a look that suggested she'd better agree and anything else was bullshit.

"I know that," she shrugged again and added, "but now other women might get that message if I wear that designer's dresses."

"Hmm," Was the only response she got on that subject before Olivia prepped her for their next appointment.

The rest of the week was a blur of shopping, fittings, and appointments for hair, make-up, and nails. While she didn't do anything too drastic with her nails, she did end up getting her hair cut, dyed, and styled to be a little more on trend. She now sported honey-blond hair that was much richer in color than her original strawberry blond tresses had ever been. Not to mention the salon had worked their magic to make it look much shinier and healthier. Every time she caught a glimpse of herself in a mirror, she couldn't help but smile. Each appointment left her feeling more confident in her looks and she didn't care if that made her seem conceited. However, all of the pampering was more attention than

Courtney was used to getting, and she was glad that Olivia was there to help her stand her ground when she didn't agree with a fashion suggestion.

She had to remind herself often that Olivia wasn't a friend but was being paid to be there. Having a personal assistant was a weird experience. Especially someone as easy-going and fun as Olivia. Courtney didn't want to feel like she was asking Olivia for anything outside the scope of her job responsibilities.

On Thursday, Courtney found herself deciding to purchase several little black dresses that were a little more daring than she was used to, but only after a prompt from Olivia. Only then did she finally force herself to ask Olivia something she'd been thinking about for most of the week.

"Olivia, does it bother you that you're here with me rather than doing stuff for Bo? I mean, you worked really hard for your position, and now you're here with some nobody, walking me through how to politely tell somebody no seven times."

"Eight if you count that damn lime green dress."

"Ugh, true," Courtney laughed then sobered. "You're changing the subject."

"I mean, honestly, Courtney, this week has been kinda fun. I don't do this stuff with Bo. He has fittings occasionally, but I only set them up. I don't go with him. I was a little surprised at first that Bo assigned me to you, but I'm truly glad he did." She leaned in and mock whispered, "You should hear how Bo's other assistant has complained about not getting this assignment. Trust me when I say you would not enjoy Diana's company."

Olivia's phone buzzed then, distracting her. When she checked the message, her eyebrows climbed her forehead. "Oh! Looks like we need to get another outfit."

"What? Why?"

"You've just been invited for dinner tonight with Bo. Shit." She put a hand to her chin, thinking, "None of your dresses will be ready before tomorrow. Agh, Bo. Why are you always throwing wrenches in my plans?"

Courtney was puzzled and a little panicked. "Why would he want to have dinner with *me*? Doesn't he have more important people to meet with?" Her voice rose as she spoke until it was little more than a squeak.

"Whoa, calm down. He just wants dinner. He's not proposing or wanting you to hop in his bed. He might run the biggest sex industry in the world, but he's not really a fast mover. I'm sure he just wants to meet you."

Courtney nodded but Olivia wasn't watching as she was furiously texting someone. Courtney wasn't so sure about Bo. The man had remembered her cat's name after one call. Who did that? "What will we talk about?"

"You, most likely," Olivia said, not looking up, which meant she missed the mortification on Courtney's face. "He's not big on talking about himself."

"What does he like? What are his interests? I need something to talk about with him, Olivia. I'm not that exciting that I can talk about myself for a whole dinner!"

Courtney's rising panic finally got Olivia's attention. "Whoa, easy there. It's going to be fine. He likes fast cars and boating and has a weird thing for horror movies."

"What? Horror movies? Really?"

"Yes, really." She pointed a finger at Courtney. "And if you tell him I told you that, you'll end up wearing that awful lime green dress tonight. Now let me work for a minute to find you something suitable to wear." She took another five minutes and finally said, "Got it."

She turned the phone to Courtney, a devilish twinkle in her eyes. "You're gonna look hot as hell in this. Maybe he *will* want to take you to bed tonight."

* * *

SEVERAL HOURS and a hair and nail appointment later, Courtney emerged from a black SUV that she'd finally let Olivia call for her. Courtney was trying not to spend all her money in the week leading up to her trip, but she caved on the SUV after Olivia explained that it was easier to get out of a tall vehicle than from a regular taxi that was low to the ground when wearing such a revealing dress.

She halted on the sidewalk when she spotted her date.

THE Bo Ryans was waiting for her outside the restaurant. He was speaking with the host at the outdoor podium and had his back to Courtney.

"You can do this," she whispered, then forced herself to keep walking in the high heels that Olivia had insisted she wear. The host looked up and gave Courtney a onceover in her tight-fitting maroon dress. It had cap sleaves that were basically off the shoulder and a sweetheart neckline that was a little more daring than Courtney was used to. At least the little ruffle of extra material that cut diagonally across the tight skirt of the dress had given her something to nervously play with on the ride over.

"Mr. Ryans?" Courtney said, glad her voice didn't waver or break as she spoke.

He turned and gave her that million-dollar smile that had been in the tabloids for most of her adult life. Though Bo was only three years older than Courtney, he'd developed a reputation as appearing and acting older than he was. His sideburns showed a tiny hint of grey, and his clean-shaven face looked soft to the touch with a few smile wrinkles that somehow made him more alluring and approachable. He wore a black suit jacket that probably cost more than three months of rent on Courtney's old apartment.

And, hot damn, it looked good on him and hugged all the right spots.

"You must be Courtney." He took her hand and dropped a light kiss on the back of it. Still slightly bent over her hand, he looked up into her eyes with his hazel ones. "It's so nice to meet you in person."

"Yes," Courtney said a little breathlessly, then kicked herself. "I mean, it's nice to meet you, too."

He smiled again, though she wasn't sure if it was at her nervousness or just because it was the polite thing to do. "Let's go inside. I sat through meetings at lunch and now I'm starving."

The host led them to a table at the back of the restaurant —which meant all eyes were on them as they passed the other diners. Each table fell silent momentarily as they passed, then hushed whispers started up the moment they had moved on. It was like leaving a weird, whispering wake in an ocean of gossip.

It made Courtney want to abort the dinner, but truth be told, she was more curious about Bo Ryans than she was nervous of those whispers. Instead, she focused on not trip-ping over her own feet in the ridiculous heels she wore. At least they were sexy, she told herself.

When they'd sat down, Bo turned to Courtney. "Do you like figs?"

It was such a random question that Courtney paused before answering in a puzzled tone, "I do, actually."

"Perfect." He turned to the waiter. "We'll have an order of the figs wrapped in bacon, please, and a whiskey on the rocks for me." He turned to Courtney.

Since she hadn't had a chance to look at the drink menu yet, she ordered off the top of her head, "A whiskey sour for me, please."

When the waiter left, Bo turned to Courtney. "Yeah? A whiskey woman, huh?"

"Not straight on the rocks, but I like it with a little something sweet."

"Something sweet with something rough." He smiled again to turn his sentence into a joke rather than a creepy leer, but it still made Courtney arch an eyebrow at him.

"I'm sorry?"

His mouth opened, and he froze for a second. Courtney could almost see him playing back the line he'd just said.

"Shit. Sorry." He rubbed his face with one hand. "I'm so used to being at the Temple all the time. Such innuendos are commonplace. They aren't polite for general conversation during dinner with an acquaintance though. Please, forgive me and let me start again?"

Courtney thought it over. As much as saying she'd been on a "date" with Bo Ryans would have been fun, the idea of said date was overwhelming. She could get on board with dinner as an acquaintance though. It was a lot less intimidating.

"Sure," she finally said.

"How has your week been so far after winning the contest?"

Courtney wasn't sure if he expected her to thank him or what, but she decided to keep things honest. "It's been...interesting so far. I guess I'm kind of lucky that I lost my job when they found out about the contest because Olivia has kept me busy with fittings all week."

He frowned. "I'm sorry that happened with your job. Some people are just not open to the idea of pleasure for fun." He paused, "Was it a job you really liked? I ask because we could help you get it back if you want."

"Oh no, no. It was just a temporary job that somehow turned into three years of office work with no real options for growth." Courtney stopped herself from saying more. Bo was strangely really easy to talk to. And, bonus: he actually seemed to be listening.

She decided to take the conversation in a different direction. "Honestly, I've been having a great time shopping with Olivia this week. She's done a really great job of keeping things organized. I have no idea how I'll ever get through shopping again without her," she joked.

"I'm glad she took the assignment," Bo said. "Olivia is the best assistant I've ever had, but between you and me, she was starting to look as burned out as I felt with all the new meetings. We've been working on starting another Temple-like site here, in New York."

"Really?"

He nodded. "It's not official yet, so please don't tell anyone, but we hope to open sometime in the spring maybe. It's a little trickier to get things passed here than it was in Vegas. They really don't like the idea of having one of our towers here. I believe one of the descriptions used in my last meeting was "tower of smut.""

Courtney stifled a laugh but not quickly enough that Bo didn't catch it. "That's a terrible description," she quickly said to recover. When he smiled with her, it made her feel more at ease, so she added, "They could really do better than that. My first thought would be Sin Spire or something like that. I mean, alliteration, people." She realized what she'd said and started to blush.

Bo ignored the blush and continued the conversation so as not to draw attention to her embarrassment. "I like that. We'll have to add that to the list."

"Do you have a real name for it yet?"

He dropped his head back. "Ah, not yet. That's the other snag." When he looked at her once more, those hazel eyes seemed to pierce right through her. He started to speak but was interrupted by their drinks.

"What would you like for dinner, sir?" The waiter asked.

Courtney suddenly realized that she hadn't even glanced at the menu yet. Flustered, she quickly flipped it open and was glad to find that it was the type of restaurant where you just picked between two full courses rather than one individual meal.

"I'll have the farmer's menu. That's the one with the steak, right?" Bo said, turning his one-hundred-watt smile on the waiter.

"Yes, sir. That's the one." The waiter turned to Courtney. "And for you, miss?"

"Actually, I'd like that as well." She almost breathed a sigh of relief as the waiter disappeared again. Why was she so nervous?

There was a beat of silence while they both sipped their drinks. When she looked up, she caught him glancing away from her cleavage which was on full display in the dress Olivia had chosen. She blushed again but decided to ignore it.

"So, you were saying about the name of the new tower?"

"Oh, yes. We're stuck in limbo right now on that. The other names were easy and matched their region. Fantasy Island is on an island. Pleasure Temple is in Vegas where there are plenty of other fake temples. But what could we use for New York? My clients don't tend to be fans of the gritty New York scene. We have some ideas of word play on the whole Broadway theme, but it's not quite what I'm looking for." He looked up suddenly. "I'm sorry, here I am complaining about work. Let's talk about you. Are you excited to head to the Temple?"

"Um, yeah. I'm excited." Courtney took a drink to cover up her nervousness.

"You *sound* excited," he said with a note of sarcasm tempered by a smile.

That smile was starting to make her feel a little warm every time it was directed her way. She wondered fleetingly what he would look like under that suit and then pushed the thought away.

Down girl! You just broke up with your boyfriend!

"Sorry. I really *am* excited. Winning was just really unexpected. I mean, I entered the contest, but I've never been the type of person to win anything, you know?"

"Well, now you are." Happily, he switched subjects after taking a sip of his whiskey. "What are your hobbies, Courtney? What do you like to do?"

The sound of her name on his lips sent a little thrill up her spine. What the hell?

"Um, I'm not too terribly exciting, really. I read a lot," here she paused before deciding to play her one ace in the hole, "and I have a weird interest in old horror movies."

"Really? I'm kind of a geek when it comes to old scary movies. What's your favorite?"

"Oh man, do I have to pick just one?"

Much to Courtney's relief, they were able to keep the conversation going well after they'd finished their meals. When it was time to leave, Bo walked them out, ignoring the stares and whispers of the other patrons.

"Do you mind if we take the same car back? I'm staying at the same hotel as you. Would that be weird?"

"I think it might be weirder to get in separate cars to go to the same destination."

"Touché."

As if it had been waiting for them, a black SUV pulled up. Bo offered his hand to help Courtney step up into the tall vehicle and she took it. Though she would have done it herself if she was with Daniel, she enjoyed the feel of Bo's strong hand on hers. He wasn't overly handsy about it, which was nice.

When he got in, his knee lightly touched hers. She tried not to notice.

"Does it ever bother you?" She asked.

"What?" He turned to her, and she suddenly had the crazy image of him leaning in for a kiss. She shoved the thought away and focused on keeping her breathing steady. What was her deal tonight?

"People staring. The whispering. Doesn't it ever get to you?"

"I honestly don't even notice it anymore. I think it went in stages though. First, I liked it, then after a while, it bothered me—which is actually why I built Pleasure Temple—it let me get away from the staring while still having people around me." He paused, looking a little concerned as his eyes found hers. "Does it bother you?"

"A little." She admitted, breaking his gaze with a small self-deprecating laugh. "I guess I'm just not used to it."

"Anonymity has its perks, but from what I understand about the interest in your story, you'll soon have more notoriety. You might have to get used to it."

"Nah. I'm sure they'll forget about me in less than it takes for the news to go through its two-week cycle."

"Maybe." They pulled up to the hotel, but Courtney didn't move to get out. Bo had caught her eyes again, and this time it made her breath hitch in her chest. As her breasts rose a little with her breath, she thought she caught a flicker of more than interest in the depths of Bo's eyes. Was he going to lean in and kiss her? The idea sent a tingle of warmth through her.

Instead of a kiss, though, he only gave her a tight smile. She was surprised at the amount of disappointment she felt.

What is wrong with you? Acquaintances, remember? She thought furiously to herself.

"Dinner was really nice. Thank you for joining me." He popped the door open on his side then turned to help her down.

She'd been doing so well in her high heels all night that in that moment of scrambling to escape her unexpected interest in Bo, she plainly forgot about them. When her foot hit the ground, she stumbled and pitched forward. Bo immediately caught her, his body pressed to hers in her form-fitting dress leaving nothing to the imagination. She could feel his arousal as she pressed against him. Surprised at his interest in her, she looked up into his eyes.

She had that feeling again that he was going to press her against the side of the SUV and kiss her, but the moment was broken when he roughly said, "Not here." He kept a hand on her arm as he stepped away from her to make sure she was back on balance. The sudden loss of his hard body against hers made her feel anything but balanced though.

"You wouldn't want to be a headline tomorrow as the woman who was picked to be Bo Ryans' personal sex toy." His smile didn't take the sting out of his words, but Courtney understood what he meant.

She gave a small nod and dropped her eyes for a moment, mentally scrambling to figure out what to say. She finally settled on, "Dinner was nice. Um, thanks." She turned and hurried into the hotel to avoid any lingering looks from the staff.

That night, as she lay in bed thinking back through that moment, she thought how close she'd come to kissing Bo Ryans and how disappointed she was that it hadn't happened. She fell asleep thinking about what could have happened with Bo in the back of that SUV. She imagined him squeezing her breast. Sliding his hands down her thighs and then hiking up her tight dress.

All the while she could feel those penetrating hazel eyes…

It was a simple fantasy, but it was one of the first times she'd thought about being with anyone other than Daniel in a long time.

Maybe she'd take Claire's advice and step outside her comfort zone to partake in more of what Pleasure Temple offered than just the room's view.

CHAPTER 4

The flight to Vegas was pretty uneventful other than the experience of taking a cat through security and then sitting in first class for the first time. Dot wasn't exactly happy about being stuck in her carrier for the five-and-a-half-hour flight, but her yowls quieted once the flight reached cruising altitude. Courtney was ridiculously grateful to have Olivia helping her through the trip. She seemed able to defuse any situation.

When they arrived at the Vegas airport, Olivia directed them to a car outside, then they both waited as a hired porter brought their bags out. This was a level of luxury that Courtney wasn't used to.

"Do you always travel like this?" Courtney asked.

"No. Usually I ride with Bo on his private plane, but he had a meeting he had to fly out early for this morning. We couldn't catch a ride with him since your dresses weren't ready."

"Oh. Sorry."

"Hey, don't be sorry. It's not your fault. If he hadn't had that meeting, he would have waited for us, and we'd have ridden with him. It would probably have been a whole lot easier for Dot, that's for sure."

Courtney wasn't so sure about this sudden meeting. She had a feeling it had more to do with their almost-kiss, but she kept it to herself. Maybe she was making it out to be more than it was. What would a freakin' billionaire want with somebody like her anyways? She was just a tourist, really, when it came to the life of the rich and famous. In three months, she'd be gone from the Temple and his life.

In fact, there really wasn't any reason to think she'd actually run into Bo again during her stay at the Temple. The place was huge. She could only assume that her room would be far away from his.

For some reason that just made her feel depressed. To distract herself, she kept her face glued to the window, looking at all the Vegas sights as they passed.

"Ooh, Caesar's Palace!" She said, suddenly feeling a little more excited. She was on vacation, damn it. Why not enjoy it?

Olivia looked up. "We have a room set up like that. People in togas pretending to be gods and goddesses. It's more a group kind of thing though...I'm not sure you'd like it."

Courtney wrinkled her nose. "Yeah. Maybe not."

"Don't worry," Olivia said, "if you do decide to take part in anything, we have some pretty sophisticated ways of figuring out what you may or may not like without throwing you into a room full of dicks, whips, and chains."

With a laugh Courtney said, "I guess that's good to hear." She was nervous about this big move and what it was going to be like at the Temple. The rest of the scenery outside flew by as she daydreamed.

Before Courtney felt she was ready, they'd arrived at their destination. Rather than stopping out front like Courtney had expected, they drove into a parking garage at the bottom of the Temple.

The driver parked near a bank of elevators where two men in black bellhop uniforms and another man in a tailored suit waited for them. The man held a tablet and gave Olivia a smile as they got out. The two bellhops immediately began unloading the bags from the back. Courtney hauled Dot's carrier out from where it had been at her feet and followed behind Olivia, who paused in front of the man in the tailored suit.

"William. Everything in order?" Olivia asked, holding out her hand.

William handed her the tablet then waved a key in front of a scanner on the wall above the elevator call buttons. This caused the buttons to light up, and he hit the up button. The elevator doors slid open, and Courtney followed Olivia and the man inside.

"Everything is in order," he said and waved the card in front of another scanner in the elevator that was next to the bank of buttons. Like outside, the buttons lit up, and he punched one of them before handing Olivia the key card.

Courtney caught Olivia's eyebrow quirk in surprise at the floor William had selected. She watched with growing curiosity as Olivia looked questioningly at the man. He shrugged as if to say, "I don't make the rules here."

Olivia gave a small shake of her head, then the moment of silent communication between them seemed to have passed. The elevator doors slid closed, and suddenly they were whisked upwards.

What was that about? Courtney wondered.

As if the moment had never happened, William picked the conversation back up again. "I mean, the dragon lady decided to peek in on me to make sure everything was being taken care of," here he rolled his eyes.

That was the second time Courtney had heard Diana being referred to negatively. She was starting to dread actually meeting the woman.

Olivia's only response to that was to shake her head before glancing back down at the tablet again. "Everything looks good." She looked back up and gave William a genuine smile. "Thanks for keeping an eye on things while I was gone. Keep this up and you'll take my position in no time."

He scoffed, "Hardly. You know Bo's never going to take on a *man* as his personal assistant." He suddenly leaned around Olivia to acknowledge Courtney. "You must be Courtney. Pleasure to meet you. Olivia's told me so much about you. It's really a pity she couldn't talk you into that lime dress."

Courtney made a face and he laughed.

"I'm just kidding. It sounded hideous. Whoever did that to that poor piece of fabric should bear the punishment of wearing it."

He shook Courtney's hand, then whipped out another keycard that he waved in front of the scanner before hitting the button for floor twenty-two. The elevator stopped a moment later, and William turned to Olivia.

"I'm off to prep the siddie room for you ladies. See you later!" He waved as the elevator doors shut.

Courtney had been researching Pleasure Temple and had read one account that said the higher up the room was in the Temple, the more money that patron had. Her eyes found the top floor, level forty.

Was that where Bo's penthouse was? She wondered and noted that the button under that for floor thirty-nine was the one William had hit when he'd first gotten on the elevator. Surely that wasn't where her rooms were? Maybe they were going somewhere else first.

Olivia interrupted her worried thoughts. "The men

downstairs will take care of our bags. I want to show you your room and get Dot settled. Then, if you're feeling up to it, I'll show you around."

"Sounds good. Could we maybe grab a coffee before the tour?"

"You read my mind. The coffee on the plane was terrible, wasn't it? You'll love the coffee here. Bo has it flown in from the island." When Courtney just raised an eyebrow in confusion, Olivia explained, "Oh, the island as in Fantasy Island. There's more going on there than just orgies. Bo purchased several coffee fields there before they could be snatched up by the big coffee companies. He wanted to keep the local economy going so that it didn't just depend on the tourism industry that Fantasy Island created. He kept the staff there local and pays them about three times what they would get from other coffee farms. He also gives all their kids scholarships."

Courtney couldn't tell if Olivia was just used to rattling off positive PR blurbs for her boss or if she was just proud to share Bo's work.

"Nice. I look forward to trying it." She hesitated, not sure what kind of questions she was allowed to ask. "Um, William mentioned something about a siddie room? What's that?"

"Hopefully we'll get to that today. It's actually SIDI and stands for Sexual Interest and Desire Inventory. Basically, it's a few different tests that help determine what kinds of activities you'll enjoy while you're here. Everyone just calls it SIDI for short."

"Oh." Somehow that wasn't quite as exciting. In fact, tests to figure out what she might enjoy sexually sounded downright terrifying.

The elevator continued to rise. Courtney was about to ask just how high up her rooms were going to be when the elevator stopped at floor thirty-two. Olivia frowned.

The doors opened to reveal Bo standing there in a button-down shirt and khakis. He seemed surprised to see Courtney. She wondered if he felt that same tingle she did when their eyes met.

"Olivia, I see you two made it to the Temple." He stepped onto the elevator and leaned back against the wall. "Welcome, Courtney. I hope you'll enjoy your stay here."

"I'm sure I will," Courtney quickly said around a neutral smile. She stole a glance at Olivia and was surprised to find the woman was still frowning at her boss.

"What's got you on level thirty-two, Bo?" Olivia asked.

"A little something new I cooked up while you were gone. Oh, come on. Don't be mad. I can have ideas without you. Hell, you might even like it."

"What is it?"

Courtney thought Olivia was trying hard not to cross her arms in annoyance at her boss. She kind of liked the way these two worked together.

"Go to level thirty-two on your vacation and you'll see."

"My vacation? You know I don't have one of those lined up for the next few months, Bo."

"Actually, after you show Courtney around, I've scheduled you to take a sort of mini vacation on the house. Courtney might still have questions, so I'd like you to be available for her, but other than that, your time is your own."

Olivia looked like she was waiting for the other shoe to drop. "What if I want to go somewhere else for vacation?"

"Then by all means, go. I can always assign Diana to help Courtney with whatever she needs."

Olivia gave Bo a look of obvious distaste. "That's blackmail."

"Is it?" His smile was deliciously mischievous.

"Fine, I would have just vacationed here anyways."

"Are you sure?" Courtney asked. "I'm sure I could get

along by myself just fine. And I could probably survive asking this Diana woman for help."

Olivia and Bo both looked at her, then laughed. It stung a little, but Bo quickly sobered. "I'm sorry. We're not laughing at you. Just trust us that you don't want to deal with Diana."

"You could probably handle her," Olivia added, "but she'll still try to swallow your soul and then eat Dot as dessert."

Courtney unconsciously clutched Dot's carrier closer to her chest. The cat was the only real piece of her old life she'd brought with her, and she loved Dot dearly, even if the cat did occasionally throw up in Courtney's shoes when she was mad about something.

"If you dislike her so much, why don't you just replace her?" She asked.

"She's the best in the business," Olivia said at the same time that Bo said, "She's great at her job." They looked at each other and grinned.

"Alright, enough bullshitting," Olivia said. "Are you going up to your office?"

"Yes, I was on my way there, mother."

He swiped his card against the scanner and hit the button for floor forty. The elevator started up again, and this time they continued all the way up to the second-to-the-last floor uninterrupted.

That meant Courtney's rooms were one level below Bo's office. She wasn't sure how she felt about that. What did it mean that her rooms were so high up in the Temple? Shouldn't they have given her rooms to someone who could actually pay for them? Was that why Olivia and William had shared that silent exchange earlier? Because her rooms were so high up or because she'd been placed so close to Bo?

The elevator finally stopped, and she was thankful to be released from the tight space.

"This is us," Olivia told her.

Courtney turned to Bo before following Olivia off the elevator. "Thanks for the welcome. See you around."

The doors closed on his smile.

Now by himself in the elevator, Bo quietly murmured, "Yes, I hope you will."

Oblivious to Bo's wishes, Courtney followed Olivia down a white, sterile yet inviting hallway all the way to its end. So far, the building looked like what she might have expected the inside of an iPad to look like: sleek, sophisticated, and expensive.

Courtney hoisted Dot up a little where the cat carrier was starting to slip.

"We're almost there," Olivia reassured her. "You won't have to take this route every day. There's another elevator near your room that will be easier for daily use. The one we took was just one that goes all the way down to the parking garage."

Courtney almost asked if Bo took those other elevators as well or if he just took the one they'd been on, but she bit her tongue. She didn't need to put her feelings on blast like that. Honestly, she wasn't even sure what those feelings for Bo were other than lust. Maybe she was just bouncing back from Daniel.

"Here we are."

Olivia stopped in front of a sleek white door that was so similar to the surrounding walls that it was almost camouflaged. The only things that made it stand out were that it was recessed into the wall and it had a small white box to its right. Olivia swiped the same card under the box that she'd used in the elevator.

The door slid into the wall like a futuristic spaceship. As Olivia stepped through the opening, lights automatically came on to reveal a small foyer with a modern wooden table.

Carefully enunciating, Olivia said, "Control: Lights on, one-hundred percent. Curtains, open."

The rest of the "room" lit up to reveal a not just a room, but a full-sized apartment, complete with a small kitchen.

Courtney followed Olivia in, doing her best to keep her mouth shut rather than gaping in awe.

"Welcome to your home for the next three months!" Olivia said, twirling dramatically toward Courtney.

Courtney stepped further into the suite. It had an open floor plan, high ceilings, and seemed filled with natural light. It was tastefully styled with understated decor that didn't look that exciting until you looked a little closer. A light blue sofa broke up the living room from the kitchen space. Facing the sofa were two beige reading chairs that Courtney felt ready to sink into with a great book. Behind the chairs was a small electric fireplace. A cat bed sat in front of it.

The bed reminded Courtney about Dot, and she put the carrier on the floor. A glance at the front door reassured Courtney that it had closed behind her, so she let the poor cat out of her carrier.

Dot darted out and then slammed to a halt at the unfamiliar surroundings. Hesitantly, the cat began to slink around the room, sniffing everything and inspecting her new home.

"She seems to be doing alright," Olivia said. "Here, let me show you the bedroom." She turned right and walked through a short hallway that had a little storage closet. Past that was the bedroom door which Olivia threw open.

It was just as airy and light as the rest of the suite. The bedspread was white with a giant yellow flower printed on it. Courtney thought it would be interesting to sleep in a king-sized bed by herself. Maybe she wouldn't end up with Dot smashed against her side or putting her arm to sleep by laying on it.

Probably not though.

In the corner was a vanity table with a bright yellow chair where she could put makeup on. To her immediate right was a full-size walk-in closet, and past that was the door to the bathroom. Olivia took her in the closet first, flipping on the light and revealing the bare shelves.

Courtney wasn't sure what to say. The closet seemed bigger than her bedroom had been in the city. Did she really have enough clothes to even start filling it?

Perhaps worried that Courtney was quiet out of concern for the empty state of the closet, Olivia explained, "It's empty now, but all the clothes and accessories we bought in New York will arrive later and will be put away by staff."

"Oh, I can put my clothes away. It's not a problem. Plus, that way the staff won't have to worry about Dot trying to escape." Courtney said.

"Nonsense," Olivia spun to Courtney. "You're living a life of luxury now. And people who live a life of luxury *do not* put their own clothes away." She softened her statement with a smile. "Besides, all of the staff who are assigned to your room are aware of Dot. They'll be careful not to let her out of the room when they put your clothes away and when they visit for turndown service. And if she does somehow manage to escape, she'd only make it to the hallway."

Before Courtney could respond, Olivia had moved on to the bathroom.

The floor and walls in the large bathroom were all marble shot through with gold. A long marble counter with cabinets underneath and two sinks above an almost wall-length mirror took up the left side of the room. A deep soaker tub sat on the other side, and an enclosed space held the toilet. Courtney noted that the toilet was also a bidet. On the far wall was a large, walk-in shower with multiple showerheads on both the ceiling and walls of the marble stall.

"The shower is digital, so you turn it on with this." She picked up a remote from the counter. "It's also a steam shower which makes things a little more fun when you're not alone."

Courtney was glad Olivia didn't add any jokes to that last bit. She'd tried showering with Daniel once thinking it would be sexy, but he'd just hogged all the hot water leaving her cold and shivering. Not exactly a pleasurable experience.

"Everything else in here is self-explanatory," Olivia said, breaking Courtney out of her reverie. "Towels are in here." She opened a cabinet on one side of the sink. "You can store your toiletries in that one." She pointed at the other stack of cabinets on the opposite side of the sink.

As they returned to the bedroom, Olivia continued explaining, "Staff will come in twice a week on a day and time of your choice to clean the whole suite and provide you with clean linens. They'll also set up any equipment you've requested."

Olivia stopped in front of one of the tall dressers and opened the top cabinet. "The bedroom TV is in here, and you can also access the apartment speaker system and On Call System or OCS from here as well."

"On Call System?" Courtney asked, finally finding her voice while she watched Dot enter the bedroom and start examining the bed. *That didn't take long*, she thought.

"I'll explain that in a minute, but first," She walked over and picked up a small pink box from the makeup vanity and returned to Courtney. It opened on hinges like a jewelry box, and she lifted out a thin smartwatch. "This will give you access to this apartment as well as the other areas we'll visit today. Your new bank account with your contest winnings is also tied to this, so you can use it like a credit card anywhere within the building. It also works as a fitness and emotions tracker."

Courtney raised an eyebrow. "It can track emotions?"

"To a certain extent. It's really tracking your heart rate more than anything else, but it's pretty sensitive and has been found to be fairly accurate." She held the smartwatch out and Courtney complied, letting Olivia put the watch on her. Once on, Olivia added, "It's also voice activated, so we're going to set that up now." She pushed a button on the side and held up a card from the box, whispering, "Say these words clearly into the watch."

"I am Courtney Bliss. I live in room 3901 of Pleasure Temple."

The watch beeped.

"Good. Next, we'll set up your safe word. Come on."

"My what?"

Olivia just smiled and beckoned Courtney to follow her out of the bedroom and back to the foyer. Here, she paused at a screen embedded in the wall that Courtney had completely missed when they'd entered the suite. Underneath the screen was a smaller sliding door that had a glowing green button to the right side.

"Tell it, 'OCS on,'" Olivia said.

"Um, OCS on."

The screen immediately lit up with the pyramid logo for Pleasure Temple which dissolved into a screen full of icons.

"This is the On Call System—OCS for short. This is kind of the bread and butter of this whole operation. You can use it to request room service or a partner for the night." Olivia clicked on the heart icon, and it pulled up a new screen. "See? You can select a partner by their physical characteristics or by their sexual interests. Mostly, these partners are other guests here at pleasure temple, but we do have a few employees here who specialize in specific kinds of pleasure like BDSM. It allows us to have more control of the environment for our guests and keeps everyone safe.

Once you select a partner, you can set a day and time for your tryst."

Olivia's tone was so matter of fact that it was difficult for Courtney to feel too awkward about the fact that she was talking about choosing sexual partners. Then again, was this really so different from some of the dating apps out there? At least here, there was no beating around the bush about what you were meeting up for.

"It's important that, no matter who you decide to partner with, that you have a safe word during your stay. Make sure it's something you're not going to accidentally say during conversation because, as you'll see in a second, the whole system responds to the safe word. Say the word once, and you'll get flashing lights and a loud tone that lets your partner know that you're no longer comfortable with what they're doing. Say the word twice quickly, and you'll activate the lights and sound along with staff members coming to help you."

At Courtney's wide-eyed look, Olivia quickly reassured her, "It's really rare that someone needs that kind of help here. The best practice is to tell your partner you don't feel comfortable anymore, but if they're too caught up in the moment, it's nice to have more options and know that help is there if you need it." She nodded once as if that was all the explanation that Courtney would need before continuing on. "Now, we're going to set up your safe word so that I know you're all squared away. Do you have a word you want to use?"

Courtney started to say no, then realized that she had the perfect word.

"Xylophone."

"Good one. Hold on one second..." She hit a few buttons on the screen, turned and held up one finger to wait, hit another button, then pointed at Courtney.

"Xylophone," Courtney said loud and clear.

The screen lit up with a green check mark and Courtney's smartwatch vibrated.

"Excellent. That means it's accepted the new phrase. Now we'll test it." She hit another button. "Okay, go ahead."

"Xylophone."

The lights in the room suddenly flashed red and yellow while a loud tone played over the speaker system. Courtney wondered if something like that would be enough to deter someone from continuing to do something she didn't like.

Not that it mattered since she didn't really plan to get involved with anyone in that kind of way while here.

Olivia hit another button on the screen and the flashing stopped. "Okay. Moving on. If you order anything like food, sex toys, etcetera, you'll get it here." She waved at the door beneath the screen. "If the button is green, that means your request has arrived." She pushed the green button and the door slid open to reveal Courtney's small rolling suitcase and Dot's bag of toys and travel cat food.

"Oh! It's a dumbwaiter!" Courtney said.

"Exactly, but we generally just call it the delivery system." She shrugged then continued on, "If you request something that's too big to fit inside the compartment or is something that needs to be set up for you, like a sex-swing, then that will be delivered by staff at your requested time. A lot of people request room cleaning and large or complicated deliveries to be done while they're not in the suite. You don't have to leave, but I've found that it's less awkward all around if you give staff privacy to do their jobs."

"I can only imagine…" Courtney murmured still stuck on the idea of a sex swing. She'd heard of them of course, but who actually used that kind of stuff?

"Okay, I think that's everything. Why don't I give you half-an-hour to decompress with Dot?

Then we can do a quick tour and end with the SIDI. That should give William enough time to set everything up for you."

"Sounds good." Courtney forced herself to smile though she was seriously nervous about the whole testing thing.

Olivia left, and Courtney walked around the suite again after depositing her suitcase in the bedroom. This was...surreal. Her hotel in New York had been nice, but this was next level living. She ended up at the large window in the living room next to the balcony doors, looking out at the Vegas strip and the crowds of people walking around down there. She'd never been to Vegas before. Maybe she'd take a little money and try gambling. It might be fun as long as she didn't spend too much. Ten thousand dollars might seem like a lot, but she knew it could go pretty quick if she got in over her head.

A light, pleasant tone sounded from the speaker near the OCS screen. She walked over and found that it said she had an incoming call though it didn't say who the caller was.

She accepted the call and suddenly Bo's face filled the screen. Her breath caught a little in her throat. She couldn't seem to get used to speaking with this man whose face she usually saw on television or magazine covers.

"Hi Courtney. I just wanted to welcome you again to the Temple. I was in a bit of a rush back there and didn't feel like it was a proper welcome."

"Oh, no. It was fine," Courtney said, putting on a smile she hoped wasn't too nervous.

"I wondered if there was anything in particular that you wished to do while you were here?"

Courtney hesitated, and Bo immediately realized the question sounded like he meant sexually. His face reddened slightly which was...alarming. He was supposed to be Bo

Ryans, the unflappable billionaire. Surely, she wasn't making him feel flustered?

"I mean," he quickly explained, "I wasn't sure if you'd been to Vegas before or not. I just wondered if there were any tourist attractions you might be interested to visit. We have agreements with most of the surrounding hotels for seats at their shows and performances."

Courtney's smile lost its nervous edge. "That would be wonderful! I've never been here and was just thinking that it might be fun to see *Pirates of Penzance*. I've also never actually gambled before, so I'd like to try that. Not a lot, of course, but it's the Vegas experience right?"

"That it is," Bo said, an idea forming in his mind that he had no business or time to make happen, yet he found himself offering anyways. "How about a showing tomorrow night? I'm sure we can scrounge up some tickets."

"That would be great! But only if it's no trouble. I can wait for another night if the tickets are difficult to get."

He put his hand to his chin in thought. The move made him seem a little more personable to Courtney.

"I'm not sure if you realize, but the news is still caught up in your story. It might be difficult for you to go to one of the casinos with the general public. We do have some tables here that you could try your hand at, with or without the real betting aspect. Up to you. I'm not a fan of slot machines—it's just mindless betting on luck if you ask me—but if you'd like to try them, maybe we could set up a more private room at one of the casinos?"

"Oh, I'm sure people won't be that excited by me going to a casino," she said, and for a brief moment, forgot who she was talking to and fell into normal conversation. "I might take you up on the offer to practice other types of gambling though, like blackjack or poker, before I try them at a real casino and end up losing my shirt." As she finished speaking, she suddenly remembered who she was talking to and clamped her mouth shut before she could say anything else, afraid of looking like a babbling idiot.

Bo isn't your friend, she firmly reminded herself. *He's just doing the big CEO thing because you won his contest. He'll forget about you by next week.*

"I'm sure you'd be fine at the card tables, but I'll set something up."

"Thank you. I really appreciate it," Courtney said, trying for a more businesslike approach.

Bo paused at her new tone, wondering if he'd somehow offended her or if she was just trying to put some distance between them. Maybe she wasn't as interested in him as he'd thought? He could have sworn they'd both had the same feelings when he'd held her against him after she'd stumbled out of their shared car the other night in New York. Maybe he'd been wrong?

Now it was his turn to force a smile in order to hide his confusion. "Great. I'll set up some gambling sessions with one of our staff members. It will appear on your calendar in the next few hours. You can just adjust the schedule if it doesn't work for you." He paused again, then decided to go for it. "I'm sure I can find tickets for tomorrow night's showing of *Pirates*. Go ahead and plan on it."

"Great!" Courtney said.

"Good. It's a date." While his words sent little alarm bells off in Courtney's head, his smile sent warm tingles through her. "Oh," he added before she could respond, "I thought I'd send up a welcome gift. What kind of person would I be if I didn't welcome my new guest?"

His grin turned mischievous as he signed off, leaving Courtney staring at the screen.

* * *

IN HIS OFFICE, Bo texted Diana to clear his schedule for the following evening. Should he take Courtney to dinner, too? He wavered. If this was truly a real date, he would take her somewhere nice where they could be appropriately dressed for the show afterwards. In his mind, this was their second date, but what if Courtney didn't feel the same? What if she was just humoring him because he was the man with the money? Maybe she was afraid he'd take away her contest winnings if she didn't comply.

In the last few years, Bo had been looking for a real relationship and had been repeatedly disappointed when it felt as though many of the women he'd dated had only found him interesting because of his money and power. He thought he'd found something real with his most recent ex-girlfriend, Kitty, but things with her had ended badly to put it mildly. He wanted someone who shared the same interests as him. Someone he could talk to. He liked Courtney but wasn't sure if she felt the same about him. Plus, she seemed a bit overwhelmed by him. He could only hope she'd get used to him.

And what better way to have her get used to him than to set up a second date?

He started making dinner date arrangements while simultaneously preparing himself for the severe chewing out he knew he'd get once Diana learned that he planned to ditch the schedule she'd painstakingly set up for him.

* * *

IN HER ROOM, Courtney still stood rooted to the spot. A date? Had he said it was a date? Wait. Was he going to the show with her...like a real date?

She jumped when the speakers chirped to announce a delivery and had to take a moment to gather herself before hitting the button to open the small delivery door.

Inside was a silver tray with a bottle of red wine, choco-late covered strawberries, and—Courtney laughed at the last thing—a cat toy. She pulled everything out and set it on the dining table that stood between the kitchen island and the couch.

Dot stared at her as if knowing that Courtney was holding something back from her. She threw the small toy for the curious cat who walked snootily over to inspect the toy before beginning to rub herself all over the catnip-filled toy.

"Well, he knows how to make Dot purr, that's for sure."

Now I just have to keep from rubbing myself all over Bo... Courtney thought with a delicious shiver.

Just then Olivia's face popped up on the screen with the words, "front door" over the top. Courtney hurried over to the door and slapped the button to open it.

Olivia's smile shifted to concern when she saw Court-ney's panic.

"What's wrong?"

"I think...I think I just set up a date with Bo for tomorrow night."

CHAPTER 5

*O*nce Courtney knew what the plan was for the next evening, she was able to partially calm down. She now sat poolside with Olivia, sipping a tropical drink during a pause in Olivia's tour of the building. Her bare feet dangled in the warm pool water, and she couldn't help but admire her perfectly manicured toenails.

Before leaving the suite, Olivia had ordered two coffees sent to Courtney's room via the OCS system. Courtney was grateful for the caffeine hit, especially since they then had to spend time preparing for her unplanned date with Bo before going on a tour of the building. Olivia helped Courtney pick out an appropriate outfit for the upcoming date—which she was definitely *not* nervous about—and also showed Courtney how to schedule hair and makeup staff to come to her room to help her prepare for her night out.

It still struck Courtney as a little surreal to have all this help. She didn't want to get so used to it that she would wind up feeling helpless when she left in three months and no longer had staff there to do her hair. A part of her wondered if she should even be using such services. Who was she to have people doing her hair and makeup just for a date?

Then again, when was she ever going to get the chance to be this pampered again in her life? She did draw the line at having her nails done again since they still looked fine from the previous manicure.

The first stop on Olivia's tour was the Temple's gym. It was an entire floor of the building dedicated just to physical and mental wellness activities. Various exercise machines lined the walls and had barriers between them to provide an illusion of privacy. There was a basketball court with a running track above it, not unlike the one Courtney had used occasionally at her local gym. There were options for one-on-one personal training and a variety of group classes Courtney could schedule to take like yoga, Pilates, or spin class.

Courtney felt a little reassured when Olivia explained that the group classes were open to all staff for free. She wasn't sure she'd feel comfortable taking classes with the rich and famous.

Best of all, everything could be scheduled right from the OCS in her room.

The floor above the gym was dedicated to a spa with massage and other offerings Courtney thought she might like to try.

Looks like I'll have some things to go do outside my room after all, she thought with an inward smile as she glanced at the list of services there.

The best floor was the next one above the spa. It was a library filled with physical books and other items she could borrow anytime.

"You can check out anything here—from kitchen appliances if you fancy dabbling in the culinary scene, to puzzles, to an e-reader with unlimited book access," Olivia explained.

Olivia had then taken her down to the second floor where they now sat around the outdoor pool. The space was meticulously landscaped to make guests feel as if they were in a tropical oasis. Palm trees masked the concrete buildings and created privacy between the small, two-person cabanas set up in sandy areas. Instead of concrete, the walkways were built out of faux wood. The best part was the saltwater pool which had a beautiful blue ocean mosaic. There was even a bar where she could have an afternoon Mai Tai or whatever her heart desired.

It truly felt like a tropical oasis.

In that moment, the only thing Courtney was drinking in was a sexy cabana staff member who only wore a Hawaiian lei for a shirt. He was well-muscled and clearly hand-picked for the job.

Down girl, she told herself. *He's a staff member.*

Olivia saw the look Courtney gave the man and quietly, so only the two of them could hear, said, "That's Sebastian. He only works the pool part time to show off his wares to the guests."

It took Courtney a moment to realize what Olivia was saying. "Wait, is his other job…?"

"Yup." Olivia smiled and waved at the man as he handed a pink drink across the bar to a woman in a white bathing suit. "He's not a bad place to start if you want to go exploring. Not very imaginative, mind you," she shrugged, "but fun, nonetheless."

"Huh." Was the only response Courtney could muster before she realized she was openly ogling the man. She was grateful when Olivia changed the subject so she would stop considering her options with Sebastian.

"The cabanas can be reserved for a private massage if you'd like to get out of the spa—all booked from your OCS."

"That thing really is the backbone of this place, huh?"

Olivia finished her drink then smiled as Courtney did the same. "It is. I can't imagine how this place would run without it. We could book things using staff and other systems, but the privacy that using the OCS offers is really what makes this place so alluring. I mean, imagine having to ask, in person, to have anal beads sent to your room. Or worse," she made a face, "having to play twenty questions with a different partner every night to figure out what they like and don't like in bed. Or out of bed," she added thoughtfully.

Courtney laughed and set her drink down. After a moment of staring off into the depths of the pool, she asked, "Doesn't this system kind of negate the idea of small talk and getting to know someone?"

"It could, I guess, if people didn't bother with relationships outside the Temple. Then again, I might not have bothered with some of the partners I've had here if I'd had conversations with them first." She jerked her head back at the bartender. "Like Sebastian over there? Great to look at, fun to touch, but not the sharpest tool in the shed."

Courtney snorted in laughter and had to look away from the bartender. They sat for a few more minutes, enjoying the quiet of the pool. It was a much-needed break after the noise and stress of traveling.

"Ready to move on?" Olivia finally asked.

"I guess so," Courtney sighed dramatically, then smiled to show she was joking.

"What if there's food involved?"

As if in response, Courtney felt and heard her stomach rumble. Olivia raised a brow to show she'd heard it too.

"I'll take that as a yes."

A few minutes later, Courtney and Olivia sat at a table in a small public cafeteria. Olivia had walked Courtney through the process of grabbing a quick meal from one of the three food vendors or from the salad bar. They'd both started with salads and were now finishing their paninis.

"This area is usually only open to Temple staff, but Bo has made it clear that you can come here anytime it's open."

"So other guests don't come here?"

Olivia shook her head, quickly finishing the last bite of her panini. "No," she said when she'd finished chewing. "Bo feels it's important to let staff truly be on break, so no other guests are allowed down here. Well," She paused, wiping her mouth with a napkin, "that's not entirely true. The other contest winner can come down here as well."

Courtney had completely forgotten about the other contest winner. She started to ask about him but decided she had a more pressing question.

"So why make the exception for us?"

"The other guests aren't allowed down here because they would most likely make demands of the staff who are supposed to be on break here. My guess is that Bo isn't worried you'll do that."

Courtney nodded, thinking it over. He wasn't wrong. She couldn't imagine asking someone on their meal break to go back to work just because she needed something. Nothing was that pressing. It helped that she, herself, had been forced to deal with demanding clients and a horrible boss who never set boundaries when it came to employees' breaks.

They bussed their own table, dropping the dishes off at a window for returns, then Olivia walked them back to the elevators. Once they were inside and the doors closed, Olivia turned to Courtney before telling the elevator where to go. "These next floors are what the guests really come here for. Most guests prefer to maintain privacy in their suites and partake in more intimate activities on the floors we're about to visit. This is where people can fulfill their wildest pleasures—within reason, of course."

Courtney held back a gulp, and Olivia scanned her card to take them to their next destination.

When the doors slid open, they stepped out into an area that was like no other Courtney had seen so far. Here, the walls were painted such a dark red that they almost appeared black except where the low lighting showed otherwise. It lent the space a permanent nighttime feel. Courtney noted a lack of windows and that the floor was black, making everything seem even darker. However, the gold of the light fixtures and wall trim somehow changed the ambience from scary to inviting and almost sensual.

Directly across from the elevator was a desk where an attractive woman in business casual attire smiled at them. A sign on the front of her desk proclaimed "Temple Pleasures" in gold lettering.

"Hey, Olivia!" She said with genuine enthusiasm before turning to Courtney. "You must be Courtney!" She stood to shake Courtney's hand. "I'm Lisa, the manager of Temple Pleasures. It's so nice to meet you! Congratulations on your win—I hope you're excited to come stay here with us!"

"Very excited, thanks," Courtney said as she shook Lisa's hand and immediately liked the woman. She didn't get that feeling of fakeness from her.

"Are you ready for Courtney's introduction to the Temple Pleasure level and her SIDI test?" Olivia asked.

"Of course! I can take over from here. Do you have anything planned for her after the SIDI?"

"Nothing yet," Olivia turned to Courtney. "Are you okay for dinner on your own?"

Though in truth, Courtney was a little nervous about not having Olivia by her side, she waved away the other woman's concerns. "Of course. I'll be fine. Thank you so much for showing me around today. I'll see you tomorrow, right?" She tried not to let the note of worry show in her voice.

"Yup. I'll let you sleep in a bit. You never know, maybe you'll find something here you want to try out tonight." With a teasing grin, Olivia got back on the elevator leaving Courtney with Lisa.

The manager called out another well-dressed staff member who took over her seat at the desk before walking Courtney through a door she unlocked with a keycard.

"Welcome to Pleasure Temple's Temple Pleasures," Lisa said in a dramatic voice that sounded like she'd said that approximately eight million times before. Then she laughed at herself. "It doesn't really make sense, does it?"

Courtney smiled and wrinkled her nose. "Not really." She was glad that Lisa was treating her as a friend or like a new employee and not like some elite guest. Though, when she thought about it, she had no idea how the woman might treat guests. Maybe this was her general spiel.

She led Courtney through another set of doors and then into a tastefully decorated office where Lisa sat on a comfortable-looking couch and patted the space beside her in invitation before picking up the tablet from the coffee table in front of her.

Courtney obediently sat and Lisa turned the tablet toward her.

"So, this isn't as scary as it sounds, I promise. We have a lot of experiences to offer our guests. Some might be for you, and some might not be to your tastes. You are, of course, welcome to try any and all of them, or leave here today and never come back to this floor."

Courtney couldn't help but laugh. "Did Olivia tell you I was nervous about all this, or do I just look that scared?"

Lisa smiled warmly. "A little of both, actually. I'm sure Olivia has probably already explained that the point of Pleasure Temple is to truly enjoy oneself and indulge in whatever you desire. There are some guests who have never ventured to this floor, but they still have a great stay. However, if you decide to try out a few experiences here, you might find yourself opening up to new possibilities. I've had guests come back who have said their visit to the Temple Pleasures level changed their lives." She shrugged. "What you do here is up to you, but it's my job to at least let you know what's available."

She sat back and brought the tablet to life. Rather than the basic icons like the OCS system that Courtney was expecting, here the screen was filled with pictures of men and women in the midst of erotic trysts. They were by no means exclusive either and were a mix of options for different genders to partner up or for three or more participants.

Courtney tried not to blush and was suddenly glad for the low lighting.

"So, once you take the SIDI assessment, you'll have a little better idea of what activities you might enjoy as well as what we'll put on the 'not interested list.' We can make that list public to other guests, too, so they know what you like. That way they can reach out if they have similar interests or desires. We can also keep your list of interests completely private. You can switch the settings to public or private at any time from the OCS in your room."

Lisa handed the tablet to Courtney and continued speaking while scrolling through the list of pleasure experiences on the screen. There were also different tabs at the top for "Positions," "Settings," and finally, "Kink." Lisa was currently scrolling through the options in the positions tab which ranged from the everyday missionary to the primal position with the man behind the woman to even more interesting positions where the woman was behind the man with a strap-on.

Oh my, Courtney thought but schooled her features so she wouldn't seem like a prude.

"Each one of the options you'll see here also show up on the OCS in your room so you can schedule a session from there. You can set up a session with our staff members as your partner, or you can put out an all call to let guests know that you're interested in sharing that experience with another guest."

Lisa switched to the "Settings" tab and began scrolling.

"Settings refers to the environment. We have quite a variety and even the appropriate costumes to go with them. Want to be a naughty librarian? You can pick the library setting and order an outfit in your size that matches that environment. Want to time travel and be a duchess who commands sexual liaison with her loyal and obedient subjects? We've got an entire throne room for that. Experiences also aren't limited to what is listed here. If you have a particular fantasy in mind, you can just send us a private message with your OCS and tell us what you desire."

Courtney was sucked into the variety of environments on display. There was a beach, the throne room Lisa had mentioned, what looked like a jungle, the inside of a spaceship, an old western saloon and brothel, a graveyard, a locker room, a cabin with a roaring fireplace and bearskin rug…the options seemed limitless.

"Your room is also listed on here if you'd prefer that, but most of our guests prefer to keep their suite to themselves for downtime."

"So Olivia mentioned," Courtney said, still looking at the pictures on the screen.

"Role-playing is, of course, par for the course."

"Of course," Courtney murmured as Lisa selected the "Kink" tab. She wasn't sure that was necessary. Courtney couldn't imagine herself taking advantage of any of these things, let alone venturing into anything kinkier than the standard missionary or woman on top positions. Daniel had once complained that she wasn't more adventurous, but he hadn't exactly had any suggestions for what to do that would be more salacious either.

Here the screen shifted to some options with pictures and others just labeled with words. The first picture was of a man as a vampire, pretending to bite the neck of a buxom woman. The next was of a woman restrained on a bed and another of a man in the same position. Another had a masked man and woman. The next was just a picture of a whip.

"Since everyone has a different definition of what they consider 'kinky,' we've created a system with ascending levels of kink. Really, level one is pretty run of the mill stuff a lot of people do in their own bedrooms at home, but for others, level one is downright unspeakable." Lisa shrugged. "As the saying goes, different strokes for different folks."

Courtney watched as Lisa continued scrolling through the options on the tablet. One made Courtney's heartbeat quicken with unexpected interest. It was of a shirtless man wearing a black leather mask and leather pants. He stood behind a blind-folded woman and pinned her hands against a stone wall with one hand while his other hand reached around to squeeze her breast. She wore a skimpy dress that was raked up to her thighs as the man took her from behind. Her expression suggested she was quite enjoying the role-play.

"You can get as kinky as you want here and can even select the level of kink you're open to. So, if you just want to be lightly restrained, it's a level one. If you want more role-play and more force, you can go up from there. It's all up to you and your partner." She paused. "Olivia helped you set up your safe word, right?"

"Yup. All set there...not that I think I'll need it." She smiled sheepishly at Lisa.

Lisa gave her a polite smile in return. "Perhaps. But like I said, for some, the Temple of Pleasures is all about exploring without guilt. If you decide you don't like something, you can stop the experience at any time. You're not here to please others—unless that's your thing. You're here to enjoy yourself."

Courtney wasn't sure how to respond to that, so she just nodded. Lisa took that as a cue to move on. She hit another button on the tablet which brought up a welcome screen.

"Okay, time for part one of the SIDI test. It's just a ques-tionnaire, so no stress. When you're finished with the ques-tionnaire, just set the tablet here on the coffee table. Then, you'll go through that door," she pointed at a door Courtney hadn't noticed at the back of the office, "to the changing room. There's a robe in there that's just for you. You can leave your bra and underwear on if you'd like, or you can be completely naked for part two. It's up to you. But the second part will consist of a sensory test. I'll explain it more when we get to it, but rest assured, no one will touch you without your permission. Okay?"

"Okay," Courtney squeaked.

Lisa got up from the couch. "I'll leave you to it then and will be back about fifteen minutes after you finish the test so that you have time to change.

Courtney nodded, and the other woman left the room.

Here we go, Courtney thought, then started the assess-ment. It took a good half-hour to get through and mostly consisted of questions using a numbered scale to ask how much she thought she'd enjoy something or how aroused she felt by thinking of specific situations or sensations. There was a section with pictures ranging from general sex to full on BDSM play. Courtney tried not to be squeamish or embarrassed by any of it and did her best to answer honestly.

She set the tablet on the coffee table when she was done. Her hands were suddenly sweaty, and her mouth was dry. Part one of the SIDI had been easy. Now she faced part two, and she wasn't too sure about it. She followed Lisa's instructions, though, and changed into the robe but decided to keep her underwear on. She left her clothes neatly folded on the same side table where she'd found the robe.

When she emerged from the changing room, Lisa was waiting for her as promised. She held out a glass of water to Courtney, who gratefully accepted it and took several sips.

"Good job completing part one. It wasn't so bad, right?" Lisa asked. She was holding the tablet Courtney had left on the coffee table. Courtney nodded in response. "Okay, so for part two, we'll go into another room."

Courtney set her water on the coffee table and followed Lisa out of the office and down the hall to a room with slightly brighter lighting but not by much. The only thing in this room was what looked like a padded dentist's chair that faced a wall-sized TV screen.

"It sort of looks like you're about to brainwash me," Courtney admitted, only partially joking.

"Not today. Maybe tomorrow," the other woman said then smiled to show that she was kidding. "Go ahead and take a seat." Courtney sat in the chair while Lisa did something on the tablet. A moment later a man and woman walked in. Both wore the same white robe that Courtney had on.

Once in the room, they took off their robes to reveal that they were stark naked underneath.

Well, that got weird quickly, Courtney thought.

"This is Franklin and Annie. They are both highly trained intimacy coaches. One of them will be administering part two of the test. It's up to you to choose which one. My recommendation is to choose the person you're most attracted to." Lisa looked down at the tablet. "Your results indicate that though you are most attracted to men, you also have some attraction toward women, so I wanted to give you both options here."

"Oh." It was news to Courtney that she might be attracted to women. "Um…" She looked at the intimacy coaches. She wasn't actually physically attracted to either of them, really, but if she had to choose, she'd be more likely to spend a night with Franklin than Annie. "Franklin."

"Thank you for your time, Annie," Lisa said. When the woman had gone, Lisa turned back to Courtney, who lay awkwardly in the chair. "With your permission, Franklin will touch you on different parts of your body to see what is the most arousing for you. Sometimes this can reveal unexpected things about ourselves, which is why we selected the best intimacy coaches possible. You're literally in good hands with Franklin. I'll just be outside."

"Okay." Courtney thought she did a good job of not squeaking at the idea of being left alone, mostly naked, with a completely naked stranger.

When it was just Franklin and Courtney in the room, he gave her a smile. "I get the feeling you're not totally comfortable with this situation. Why don't I put my robe back on while we get started?"

"That would be…helpful," Courtney finished lamely.

He donned his robe then stepped up beside Courtney. "You can tell me to stop at any time, Courtney. This is a completely safe space. Why don't we start with your hands?" He held out a hand for Courtney, and she placed her hand in his. "Good. Some people find it helpful to close their eyes and picture someone they're attracted to as the one touching them. It's what gets the most accurate sensory response."

Courtney closed her eyes.

"Now, I'm going to move my hands on different parts of your body. Don't worry. I'll be above your robe the whole time for this part." Courtney nodded. "You don't actually need to say anything during this process since the smart-watch on your wrist will track all of your body's responses and feed them into your profile."

"Okay."

As promised, Franklin began to explore her body, always keeping his hands on the outside of her robe. He moved from her hand, up her wrist, to her arm, and progressed up her shoulder, over her breast, then up to her neck. Only when his flesh touched hers at her throat did she feel any kind of response. Even then, in all honesty, she kind of felt like she was in a doctor's office. He did the same on the other side of her body then stopped.

She opened her eyes.

"Good," he told her with a soft, clinical smile. If he had appeared to be enjoying that, she couldn't tell. Which was why she agreed to his next request. "I'm going to have you stand up now and take off your robe. Is that okay?"

She nodded and did as she was asked. When she dropped her robe to the floor, he did the same, standing naked in front of her again.

"Now," he said, stepping forward and taking her hand again. "I'm going to do that same process again. Is that okay?"

She nodded and closed her eyes again.

This time, the experience of Franklin touching her body was different. Instead of doing each side individually, he used both hands to touch both sides of Courtney's body simultaneously.

When he reached the upper part of her arms, she felt her heartbeat pick up a little. He paused there, moving his hands up and down her arms. It just felt like he was trying to warm her up. Not so sexual. He must have realized this because he then slowed his movements until it was more of a sensual stroke. Courtney felt a faint bit of interest stirring within, which was funny because she'd never thought of someone stroking her arms as sensual.

"I'm going to try something else," Franklin said before he suddenly took a firmer grip on her upper arms, pulling her toward him in a more possessive move. She gasped a little, not at the suddenness of the movement but at the spike of desire that Franklin had just elicited in her. It was gone as quickly as it had come, though.

He released her arms and moved more slowly now, up, over her shoulders and across her collar bones. The sensation made her take in another little breath.

She remembered Franklin's earlier advice and imagined it was someone she knew who was touching her. Of course, the first person who came into her mind was Bo.

It's just because you're in his building, she told herself firmly.

But when she imagined that it was Bo slipping his hands down her front to gently caress her breasts, her nipples immediately hardened under her bra. From there, the hands explored her sides, her stomach, and then her thighs. Here again, she felt an uptick in her excitement when his hands brushed her waist. Like earlier, he suddenly made a possessive move, gripping her waist and pulling her to him. Courtney gasped, and a pure shock of electric need shot through her groin.

If only it were really Bo standing naked before her.

Next his hands moved from her waist to her butt. He caressed her through her underwear, then suddenly pulled her toward him again, pressing against her firmly against his naked body. She inhaled sharply as electricity lit up her groin again.

Oh my, she thought, not willing to open her eyes.

She continued to imagine it was Bo who, still keeping his hands on her body, moved to stand beside her, pushing his hard erection against her. Moving his hands around to cup her breasts over her bra.

"You can take it off," she softly whispered, surprised by her own daring.

He did, and then resumed his exploration, moving to stand behind her now, pressing his naked member against her. In her mind, it was Bo who brushed his fingers over her nipples before stopping to play lightly with them. She couldn't help herself. She groaned in response and pushed back against him, suddenly wishing he'd take off her underwear, too.

Much to her disappointment, his hands left her breasts but only so he could pull her arms overhead, carefully bending her over slightly, so her arms rested against the top of the chair. She suddenly flashed back to the picture she'd seen on the tablet, of the man taking the woman in the cave. Need rippled through her and, almost of its own volition, her body pushed back harder against him.

With one hand holding hers in the air, he slid his other around her front and down between her legs, gently touching her clitoris through the thin fabric of her underwear. She moaned this time and pushed forward against his hand as pressure began to build from his gentle movements. She was almost panting now, wanting, no—needing Bo inside her.

Suddenly he stopped and stepped away.

No! She frantically thought. Her eyes flew open to find Franklin putting his robe back on. She'd known it was him the whole time, but it was still a bit of shock and somewhat embarrassing that it wasn't Bo standing there.

Franklin held out her robe with a smile, not showing any

embarrassment in the least. "You did a great job, Courtney. I know part two can be kind of weird."

Not to mention close to just being a tease, Courtney thought but didn't say.

"Lisa will go over your results with you, but I truly think you would enjoy up to a level two or three of kink. Maybe start with masks. That way you can picture whoever you want like you just did with me. Then you can work your way up more or mix that with other fantasy experiences: a masked ball, a masked robber 'breaking into' your house." He used air quotes around the words. "Things like that. Great job," he said again. "I hope you have a wonderful stay here." And then he was gone.

It was honestly the weirdest encounter Courtney had ever had. Part of her had wanted him to stay so they could finish what they'd started, and yet another part of her felt he hadn't left the room fast enough. It was an odd conflict of feeling that Courtney wasn't used to.

Courtney had already put her robe back on when Lisa knocked then popped her head in the door. "All good?" At Courtney's nod she continued, "Good. Come on, we'll head back into my office to talk about your results and some suggestions."

When they were back on the couch in her office and Courtney had changed back into her own clothes again, Lisa held the tablet out to Courtney. "So, the things highlighted here are what your scores indicate could bring you the most pleasure."

The top thing on the list was the picture of the man taking the manacled woman from behind. The image made her flash on her imagined tryst with Bo a few seconds ago, and she felt that pang of need again.

"Really?" She managed to say in a neutral voice after

taking a sip of water from the glass she'd left in the room earlier.

"Really. Our data is almost never wrong, so some of these, as outrageous as they may seem to you right now, might actually be really pleasurable experiences. My recommendation would be to start at a level one, then, if you feel comfortable, try the next level."

Courtney cleared her throat. "Franklin suggested I could mix them up with other fantasy experiences?"

"That's also a good idea. Especially if you get bored of something." She flipped to another screen that showed different sexy outfits mostly consisting of short skirts and lingerie. "These are the types of clothes that give you the most pleasure to wear." She swiped to another page. "And these are what you might want someone else to wear."

The outfits on that page were mostly just pants or old-timey breeches. However, there was one skimpy skirt and a matching bikini top that caught Courtney's eye. She pointed at it, "Um…"

"Remember, though your results leaned more toward being attracted to men, it looks like you have some attraction to women as well. There's no judgement here. It's a safe place to explore your interests and sexuality, but you might feel more comfortable starting with a man or men as partners first before getting more adventurous. You could also start by being blindfolded with a woman or by being the recipient of pleasure from another woman. In that case, I would recommend that you partner with our highly trained staff. That way you get the best experience, and there are no hard feelings if you decide you want to stop."

She paused before continuing on, "If you're a little lost as to how to proceed, we can also create a tailor-made encounter plan for you based off of your SIDI results. These encounters would start with very light, no kink encounters and would gradually step up based off the interests we found from your assessment. A lot of people prefer this as it adds a little spice not knowing what exactly to expect in their next encounter."

She looked at Courtney for a second, clearly sensing she was hitting a limit on how much information Courtney could process in one day.

"Why don't you go back to your room and look through some of these as well as the optional fantasy experiences. Think on it, and if you want to try one, you can start with something simple. For now, we'll just leave your interests and desires to the private setting. If you decide to change your mind and want to invite some company to come play, you can switch it to public with the push of a button."

Lisa showed her out of her office and back to the elevator. When Courtney was safely back in her room, she sat on the couch for a few seconds still trying to recover from her encounter with an imaginary Bo.

Did she really want to just sit in this suite for the whole three months? Now that she'd had a taste, she wasn't so sure.

CHAPTER 6

*D*ot broke Courtney out of her reverie by reminding her that it was time for dinner. It only took Courtney a moment to find Dot's food. It had been left in a plastic container in the kitchen. There were even new food and water bowls in one of those fancy raised trays.

She petted Dot as she ate and told her, "You're living the charmed life now."

Dot was too busy with her food for a response, so Courtney decided to take the opportunity to investigate the suite. True to Olivia's word, Courtney found all her new clothes had been put away in her walk-in closet. They only took up a tiny part of the massive space. It was kind of tempting to use some of her winnings to fill up the rest of the closet.

The small suitcase that had held her regular clothes stood empty in the closet. After a quick search, she found that those clothes had been neatly put away in the bedroom bureau. Her toiletry case had been left in the bathroom by the sink.

"This is gonna take some getting used to," she said to the

empty room before realizing that just the idea of living alone was going to take some adjustment. She'd always had a roommate. She'd lived with Claire in the college dorms, then they'd moved into an apartment after college. After that, she'd moved in with Daniel and had been there ever since.

She wasn't quite sure how she felt about the idea of living alone.

If she was being honest with herself, her biggest fear in leaving Daniel, besides the fear of not having a place to live, had been the idea of being truly alone. There had always been someone else there.

And now there wasn't.

A whirring sound from the hallway was a welcome distraction from her thoughts. As she went to see what was going on now, she caught sight of something she was sure hadn't been there when she'd left for her tour earlier. There was now a cat-sized opening in the hallway closet door with a little plastic flap. She opened the full-sized door and found that it was an entrance for Dot to access a new, automated cat litter box.

"Whoa, you really are living a fancy life, Dot."

It didn't take Courtney long after that to open the bottle of wine Bo had sent up and order something for dinner using the OCS. There were so many options that she finally just went with the classic steak and mashed potatoes. She figured it would go well with the red wine anyways. Plus, she'd have plenty more opportunities to try something more adventurous in the next three months.

Her meal arrived via the delivery system within fifteen minutes of ordering and was still hot when she opened the little delivery door. There was even a bottle of steak sauce included. With the meal, a message arrived on her OCS screen that suggested she keep the steak sauce in her fridge if she planned to order more steak in the future.

Seems like a logical suggestion, she thought.

She was sitting at her table, thoroughly enjoying her meal and more than halfway through her bottle of wine when she got a call to her personal phone. She'd been so lost in thought thinking back over her day that she hadn't even bothered to retrieve her phone when she'd gotten back to her suite.

She trotted to her room and pulled her phone from the purse she'd left on the bedroom bureau. She was immediately sorry she had.

Daniel's name popped up on the read out. Instantly, she felt feelings of guilt for her encounter with Franklin and for her interest in Bo.

"You don't owe him anything," she whispered to herself, but hit the answer button anyways.

"Courtney?"

"Yup. Hi, Daniel."

"I've been calling all day! Why didn't you answer or call back?"

"Sorry," she said, then immediately kicked herself for apologizing. "I left my phone in the room while I was getting a tour."

He gave a harrumph like he didn't believe her. She decided to let it go for now.

"What's up, Daniel?"

"What's up? What's up is that I just wanted to see how your trip was so far."

"It's…good. I had a good flight. First class, actually, which was a first for me." She smiled thinking of all the firsts she'd had just in the last week alone.

"Must be nice," he said, instantly dragging her mood down and making her feel guilty again.

No, damn it. You don't have anything to feel guilty for!

"Did you want something Daniel, or are you just calling to try and make me feel bad?"

"Make you feel bad! How am *I* making *you* feel bad? You're the one who left me."

She sighed loudly to make sure he heard her annoyance. "I'll talk to you later, Daniel."

"No, wait! Don't hang up. Look, I'm sorry. This is just… really hard. I miss you, Courtney. I really do."

Her guilt flared back up. Did he really miss her? And here she was having a good time. She slowly sank into the comfortable couch with her glass of wine in one hand, pressing the phone to her ear with the other.

"I miss you, too," she somewhat reluctantly said. As the words tumbled from her mouth, she was a little surprised to realize that they weren't true. It was sort of shocking.

"Please come back, Courtney. I'm really, truly sorry. I won't take you for granted anymore. I just didn't realize what I had until you were gone."

His words were a twist of the knife in Courtney's heart. If he had said something like that before she'd left, she might have backed out of coming to Vegas.

But he hadn't, and now here she was. *And what if I actually learn more about myself while I'm here?* She wondered.

That wouldn't happen if she left now. Not if she went back to the way things were. It wasn't just the occasional, pleasureless sex she didn't want to go back to, it was realizing that she would be just as lonely living with Daniel than being here in Vegas by herself. Actually, she was pretty sure that she would feel even *more* alone if she went back now.

"I'm sorry, Daniel, but I'm going to stay. Maybe we can feel it out in three months and see if staying together is the right thing to do at that point."

There was a shocked silence on the other end of the line, followed by spluttering as Daniel tried to think of what to say. "What? How…! I'm not going to just wait around for three months for you to come back from a sex-cation!"

Courtney suddenly realized that she wasn't the only one who'd been drinking.

"And," he continued, "how dare you just walk out on our relationship! I spent years of my life with you! I thought I was going to marry you!"

That was news to Courtney. Now it was her turn to be angry. "Daniel, you've never once even brought up the idea of marriage! And anytime I even mentioned it, you would shut down the conversation like you were terrified of being locked into something with me."

"I guess that's a good thing now!" He yelled. "Glad I didn't put a ring on your finger before I found out you wanted to whore around with other men."

Fighting and confrontation always made Courtney emotional. She found herself wiping away sudden tears while fighting to control the waver in her voice. "I guess you shouldn't have given me an ultimatum then, huh? We could have stayed together, and I would have treated this as nothing more than a free vacation. I'd have been true to you, and you know it. You know me. Instead, you tried to order me not to go. You don't own me, Daniel."

"You know what? I *do* know you, and I know that you'll never do more than get to first base with any of the guys there. Not that any of them would want you anyways after they realize all you're willing to do is let them climb on top of—"

She ended the call before she heard any more of his poison. How could she have stayed with someone like that for so long?

Because you're afraid that he's right. That no one else will want you.

And there it was. Beneath that surface fear of being alone was her real, deepest fear: that no one else would love her or desire her.

She took another swig of wine, then threw her phone to the other side of the couch. Wiping tears away and feeling a new defiance mostly from liquid courage, she picked up the tablet from the coffee table and flipped through to the screen of her results. With a simple tap of a button, she made her results public, then scrolled through the different suggestions from her SIDI test.

Shoving back a wave of trepidation, she selected the experience that had turned her on the most. It was the one with the man taking the woman from behind. She also selected that he be masked and set the experience at kink level two. She set the desired encounter to immediate, selected that she didn't want to know who the other party was, and hit submit while holding her breath.

She suddenly giggled, covering her mouth with a hand to stifle the sound. "It's not like anyone is going to jump at the chance to be with you that quickly," she told herself, then settled into looking through the suggested outfits for such an encounter since she figured she'd have plenty of time. If she changed her mind when she was sober tomorrow, she could always cancel the open invitation and return her settings to private.

After some hemming and hawing over the huge selection of sexy outfits, she finally selected a bright blue silk teddy with a matching thong and requested that it be sent to her room.

She almost spilled her wine at the chime that came out of the OCS. She looked down at her tablet to find that someone had responded to her request. Her partner, a man named Raife, had set the encounter for an hour from now and suggested a neutral bedroom environment in the Temple of Pleasures.

"Holy shit!"

Dot jerked awake in the chair across the room.

"Holy. Shit," Courtney said again. Should she cancel the encounter? She wasn't ready, was she?

Daniel's words echoed in her head, *"Not that any of them will want you..."*

Now, it seemed that someone *did* want her. Someone named Raife. Would she continue being unadventurous and never try anything outside of her comfort zone? Or should she start living a little? Honestly, there was no safer place to try something new like this than in Temple Pleasures.

But what the hell would she wear? She flipped back to the list of clothes and looked at the delivery estimates. The blue teddy wouldn't be ready before her scheduled meeting with Raife.

"Shit!"

She leapt up and ran into the bedroom. Twenty minutes later, she finally decided to wear the red lingerie she'd brought from home. After a quick shower that didn't include her hair, she brushed her teeth, put on fresh makeup, pulled on the lingerie, and slipped one of the little black dresses from her recent shopping spree over the lingerie.

Looking at herself in the mirror, she *felt* sexy.

She just hoped her partner felt the same way.

Ten minutes later her hands shook as she scanned her card to open the door for the appointed location in the Temple Pleasures. The man working the front desk of the Pleasures level had been completely professional when he let her through the door and guided her to the room.

The room was simple with a four-poster bed covered in a white comforter. There was a bathroom off to the left and a plain, wooden desk against one wall with a plain wood chair. Other than that, the room was bare—

—Except, Courtney realized, for the rings mounted in the ceiling, the walls, and even two on the wooden desk.

Seeing the metal rings made Courtney reassess the situation. She started to retreat, stumbling a little on what she thought of as her tall "fuck-me" heels, but the door suddenly opened behind her. She spun to find an imposing man in the doorway, wearing a leather mask that covered most of his face, leaving his mouth and nose exposed. His chest was bare, showing off a set of six-pack abs and a rock-hard chest. His tight leather pants left little to the imagination in the size department.

"Um," Courtney said, "Raife?" The man nodded, pulled the door closed behind him, then put a finger to his lips as he stalked into the room after his prey.

In his other hand were pieces of silk material. Courtney's heartbeat quickened at the sight of the silk ties.

Maybe level two was a little much for her first encounter?

It seemed that it was too late to back out now. And honestly, as Raife slowly approached, his muscles contracting under his leather pants as he walked, Courtney wasn't sure she *wanted* to back out. She had her safe word if she needed it, right?

Raife stood awkwardly in front of her for a moment, then moving slowly so as not to scare her, he reached out and ran a hand from Courtney's shoulder, down her arm, to take her hand. The move slipped the strap of her dress down her shoulder, exposing the red lingerie underneath. Raife's eyes warmed at the sight and wonder of wonders, she thought his bulge somehow grew larger under those leather pants.

Clearly, here was someone who wanted her after all.

She closed her eyes at his touch—

Raife suddenly yanked her toward him. She let out a little yelp of surprise and opened her eyes as he pressed her against his naked chest. His hands moved down her back until they reached her butt to pull her more firmly against his member.

Courtney gasped and closed her eyes again. Suddenly his

mouth was on hers, demanding a response as one of his hands slid to her breast. Something about Raife's roughness sparked electricity through her body, and she responded, pressing her herself against his erection.

Still kissing, he slipped one of the pieces of silk over her eyes and tied it on as a blind fold before slowly walking her backwards toward the bed. When her back met one of the bedposts, he pulled his mouth away from hers and raised her arms over her head, gently pinning them against the bedpost.

"Keep them there," he ordered as a whisper in her ear before kissing her neck below her earlobe. She shivered as his hands slid down her arms, caressing her body, until they'd reached her thighs. Then in one sensual move, he slid her dress up over her head and over her upraised arms.

This is moving so fast, she thought, heart racing in anticipation.

Then his mouth was suddenly back on hers, and she could only imagine Bo and how this might feel with him. Before she could put her arms down again, he grabbed both her wrists in one of his hands and pressed himself against her again.

Sharp need rose up as he seemed to press just the right buttons, and she wrapped a leg around his waist.

He let out a little gasp of his own and pulled away again, this time to tie her hands to the bedpost. When that was done, he slowed down, taking his time now. His hands slid down, first caressing, then squeezing her breasts through the lingerie before pulling the fabric cups down and closing his mouth on one nipple while gently rubbing the other. She rocked her hips toward him, wanting more as electricity danced from her nipples to her groin. She couldn't help letting out a gaspy moan.

He pulled away again, and Courtney suddenly realized that there was something terribly erotic and exhilarating about not knowing what was going to come next. She'd given herself up to the darkness of the blindfold, and she didn't regret the pleasures it brought one bit.

His next move was to pull her hips toward him while he kissed her again, so deeply that she was left gasping for air. While they kissed, he'd reached underneath her lingerie and shimmied her thong off. Now all she wore was the scanty piece of red fabric, and even that was barely covering her.

When they met again in a kiss, he pressed his hard erection against her, still locked inside his leather pants. She felt him fumble for the zipper, and when he was free, she locked her legs around his waist again and he held her up, pushing her against the bedpost.

She gasped in surprise and pleasure as he entered her. Though she'd expected it, not being able to see what was happening was amazing. She tried to match his thrusts, wanting him to fill her up, but couldn't get much leverage.

Gently, he pulled out of her and set her down so she was standing again, though somewhat shakily and breathless. After a second, she realized he'd untied her hands from the top ring and had moved them to a lower one.

His lips found hers again as pressed his now completely naked body against hers once she was secured to a lower ring in the bed frame. His mouth left hers to kiss her neck, then her collarbone, and finally lock around her other nipple.

"Ohh. Don't stop," she said, breathlessly trying and failing to pull him toward her with her tied hands. To get him inside her once more. Instead, he pulled away.

"Shhh," he quietly said in her ear. The sensation and the message sent tingles of pleasure and anticipation down her spine.

The message was clear: He was in charge here.

As if to prove the point, he roughly spun her around, pushed her against the bed, hiked up her lingerie and entered her from behind. She gasped, and he pulled back only to thrust into her again. One of his hands snaked around to squeeze her breast while the other moved between her legs. It was almost the same move, she realized, that Franklin had used earlier.

His fingers found that sweet spot, and she groaned as their movements fell into sync. Him thrusting into her at the same time as he rubbed his finger against her clitoris. She began pushing back into him, wanting him deeper inside her as the pressure built. Just as she was about to climax, his hand slipped up to cover her mouth and stifle her cry.

For some reason, that was even more erotic to her mind. She bucked against him as the orgasm carried her away on a wave of pleasure. He came a moment later, then leaned against her, breathing hard.

After a moment, he pulled out of her and smoothed her lingerie back down. He disappeared for a moment, and it sounded to Courtney like he was putting his clothes back on. As if to prove that he was still in charge, he untied her hands and turned her to face front again before pressing her back against the bedpost for a last, lingering kiss that promised future pleasures.

He then put his mouth to her ear while her eyes were still closed from the kiss and whispered. "A pleasure, Courtney."

Her name on his lips sent a shiver down her spine, and her eyes snapped open, catching a glimpse of his roguish smile.

Before she could respond, he turned and disappeared out the door.

* * *

COURTNEY SAT in a tub full of bubbles, replaying the scene in her mind. Had she really just done that? Had she really just had sex with a complete stranger? She didn't even know what he looked like.

Then again, did it matter when the sex was that good?

She put a hand to her face and laughed. "Claire will *never* believe me," she told a disapproving Dot who glared at her from the doorway.

It had been a little while since she'd had sex, and she'd *never* had sex like *that* before, so she was a little sore. A soak in the tub, followed by lounging on the couch in a bathrobe while drinking the rest of the wine Bo had sent up was just the thing she needed.

She was just thinking of turning in early—after all, it had been a long, but very exciting day—when a message popped up on her tablet.

Raife: Being inside you was a pleasure. I'd love to do it again sometime.

Courtney caught her breath. Her first reaction to his message was embarrassed repulsion that it was so sexualized, then she thought, *What's wrong with that?* She'd just been willingly tied up and taken from behind—and had loved every second of it. It might have been different if he hadn't given as much as he got. But he'd been a very attentive...what? Lover didn't quite sound right. Maybe partner?

Instead of ignoring the message as her prudish self might once have done, Courtney took another sip of liquid courage then typed back: The pleasure was all mine. I'd love a round two. Have anything in mind?

It was a few minutes before he wrote back: I'll look over your desires, but I think I have a few ideas. Tomorrow night?

Courtney almost told him yes but remembered just before hitting send that she had a "date" with Bo tomorrow. She felt torn but knew she'd also enjoy her time at the theater, though probably not as much as she'd enjoy another session with Raife.

Before she could change her mind, she beat back her prudish nature and replied: Can't tomorrow. How about Sunday? That will give you some time to send me something to wear.

She added a winking emoji followed by an eggplant emoji. If he didn't know what that meant, he could look it up.

His response was swift. Courtney's face turned beet red.

Raife: Yum. I have just the thing in mind. I look forward to filling you up again.

And just like that, Courtney had more dates set up in two days than she'd had for most of her entire college experience.

CHAPTER 7

$\mathcal{T}$he next day flew by in a blur. Courtney ordered breakfast on the OCS, and afterwards she decided to go explore the gym. She was a little intimidated by some of the weight machines and stuck with a short stint on the elliptical.

Next time, workout first, then breakfast, she thought when she started to feel her stomach protesting the workout. On the way out, she stopped and signed up for a session with a personal trainer. It was kind of intimidating since she'd never had the money to work one-on-one with a trainer before, but since it was on the house, she figured she'd try to step outside her comfort zone.

Then again, I was pretty damn far outside my comfort zone last night, she thought with a slightly embarrassed smile.

After a quick shower back in her room, she only had a few minutes before Olivia arrived. She flipped through the OCS system, looking at outfits and potential encounters. Now that she'd already experienced one, the others didn't sound so intimidating.

Her doorbell rang, interrupting her exploration into what

the Temple had to offer, which was probably for the better since she was starting to feel the stirrings of lust again just looking at the options. She needed to be focused for the day ahead, not sit around longing for another round with Raife.

"Any exciting plans for today?" Olivia asked when Courtney opened the door.

"I was thinking of checking out a casino or two this morning." Courtney shrugged. "Maybe play some slots."

"Are you sure you want to do that? Bo sent me a message that he was setting up some private training sessions for you here."

"I know, but that's for card games. He said there weren't any slot machines here. And honestly, it's less about the gambling and more about getting the Vegas experience."

Olivia gave her a sideways look. "I'm not sure you'll get that at ten in the morning. Unless the Vegas experience you're looking for is a late morning walk of shame and watching grandma gamble all her retirement savings away on slots."

Courtney laughed. "Actually, I kind of just want to check out the casinos and see what they're like inside. Like, what's going on with that fake Eiffel tower I can see from there?" She pointed at the balcony. "If I'm gonna treat this like vacation, then I want to go see the sights."

Olivia glanced out the window but still didn't seem convinced. "Okay, but just remember that people might recognize you."

Courtney waved away the notion. "If it's really as dead out there right now as you say, then the people who would recognize me probably aren't up yet."

Olivia smiled. "True. Okay, let me request a car. If we're back here by four, then that will give you time to get ready for tonight."

Half-an-hour later they walked down the mostly quiet

strip, Courtney staring at the sights. She took some selfies in front of the Paris Hotel's Eiffel tower and then again at the Arc de Triomphe. After some cajoling, she convinced Olivia to go inside with her for crepes but only because coffee was involved.

At Caesar's Palace, Courtney gambled away ten bucks on penny slots which took about an hour. When she looked over at Olivia, she noticed the woman looked rather bored, and she started to feel bad for dragging her around all day. They left after that and grabbed some Chinese takeout for lunch at a fast-food court.

"Are you sure you're okay with this?" Courtney asked Olivia, waving her chopsticks around to indicate the food court.

"We're kind of already here. And honestly, it's been a while since I had Chinese food. It's a nice break from the Temple."

Courtney nodded and decided to ask what she'd been thinking about all day. "It's kind of weird, right, that you're being paid to hang out with me? I feel like I'm kind of wasting your time by dragging you around."

Olivia started to shrug off Courtney's concerns, but when she caught the other woman's eyes, she decided to be up front. She sighed. "It's definitely not what I'm used to doing. To tell you the truth, I was a little, ah, miffed—"

Courtney lifted an eyebrow at the PG word.

"Okay, pissed off at Bo for assigning me to you. It felt like he was punishing me for something by asking me to babysit the contest winner."

Courtney cringed at the idea that she needed a babysitter, but the truth was that if Olivia hadn't been with her in New York, she would absolutely have drowned in that sea of fittings and styling appointments. She definitely would have felt obligated to buy that terrible lime green dress. Here, though, now that she felt a little more in control of things, it *did* feel like Olivia babysitting her.

"So..." Courtney ventured, truly curious. "What happens if I don't need your help for something? Like, what would you be doing if you weren't here showing me the sights?"

"Normally, I'd be arranging Bo's schedule for some new projects—"

"Like the one in New York?"

Olivia gave her a surprised look. "He told you about that?"

"At dinner the other night in New York."

"Huh." Olivia was silent for a moment before picking up the thread of conversation again. "Anyways, I would probably be helping with that, but I'm not sure he'll assign me anything like that right now."

"You mean right now while I'm here," Courtney said, trying to keep any emotion from her voice. She didn't like the idea of being the reason that Olivia wasn't getting more interesting assignments that were more on her level.

She wasn't able to hide it from the hawk-eyed Olivia though.

"Look, don't feel bad about this. Yes, I would probably be doing something different if you weren't here, and yes, I might have been pretty pissed at the assignment initially—"

Courtney looked up from twirling the noodles around the bottom of her takeout container to give Olivia a look that said, "give me a break."

"Okay, yes, I'm still a little pissed at the assignment," Olivia amended with a small smile, "but today was a nice break from the usual hectic schedule when I'm back here in Vegas."

"But you wouldn't want to do this every day."

"Would you?"

"Not really. There's only so many sights to see. Three

months is a long time. I feel like I need to pace myself. And while it was fun having you with me today, I can also do things by myself. I mean, I lived in New York City, I think I can find my way around Vegas on my own."

"Exactly. You don't *really* need me here. And, no offense, but you don't really have much going on that you need me to schedule anything." She shrugged. "But without other assignments from Bo, I don't have much else to be doing workwise."

They were silent for a few minutes, each lost in their own thoughts. Courtney wondered how she could fix the situation while Olivia was concerned that she'd maybe said too much. Olivia was finding it easy to speak openly to Courtney after what seemed like a lifetime of working in a cutthroat environment with coworkers who wanted to stab her in the back to take her job and Bo's previous girlfriends, who were willing to cut her down to her face out of jealousy for the time she spent with her boss. Assisting Courtney was actually pleasant, and Olivia had to keep sternly reminding herself that Courtney was a client and not a friend she could be so open with. She decided it was time for a change of subject.

"Anyways, enough about me." Olivia gave Courtney a wicked grin. "What's this I see that your interest and desires are publicly displayed on the OCS? Did you change your mind about what you wanted to partake in while you're here?"

Courtney immediately turned red and ducked her head, not ready for that line of questioning. "Um, yeah. I might have tried out an, um, encounter last night."

"What? That's great, Courtney! I'm so glad you're taking advantage of being here. That's the whole point after all."

"Yeah. It was...nice." Courtney couldn't help a ridiculous

grin at the memory of Raife pushing her up against the bedpost.

"Let me know if you have any questions about anything."

Courtney gave her a look, and Olivia immediately laughed and corrected her statement. "Anything about the Temple, woman. Get your mind out of the gutter." She sobered a little then added, "But honestly, you can also talk to Lisa or any of the other staff on the Pleasure level to ask questions about that kind of thing. Or if you get bored, they can help you find something a little more exciting."

Courtney nodded and was about to ask about profiles and how she could look up Raife to see his interests and desires, but they were interrupted by a man walking past their table.

"Oh, hey! You're that chick that won the Pleasure Temple thing!" He was with a group of other guys who all looked to be in their early twenties. "Guys! This is that chick who won three months at that sex place!" He turned his attention back to Courtney and pulled out his phone. "Can I get a picture with you?"

Before Courtney could answer, the rest of his group converged on their table. One of the other men gave Courtney the full once-over, stopping for a moment to stare at her breasts. She wasn't sure exactly what he got out of that since she was fairly conservatively dressed in a red pair of cropped jeans and a high cut blouse, but he was clearly checking her out.

"What's it like in there?" He asked while another guy in the group openly leered at Courtney and Olivia. "Yeah, what's it like? Did they fuck you in the ass yet?"

Courtney pulled back in revulsion at the man's vulgar question, which was followed by his bray of laughter.

"Time to go," Olivia said under her breath. She stood and Courtney followed suit.

"Oh, come on, ladies." The vulgar one said, walking after them. "Why don't you come party with us? I bet we'd be a lot more fun than what you can get in the Temple."

Olivia paused from where she'd been texting their driver for a pickup. She looked the vulgar man up and down. Then laughed. "I don't think so. You see, we have *actual* men in the Temple. Not children pretending to be men." She smiled then pulled Courtney along in her wake.

Courtney glanced back, afraid the men might try to retaliate. The vulgar one started to follow them, but one of his friends, the one who had first identified Courtney, grabbed his arm and held him back.

Olivia tugged on Courtney's arm to keep her moving. "Come on Courtney. We need to get out of here."

Thankfully, their car wasn't far away. When they were safely in the backseat, Olivia turned to Courtney.

"Just what Bo and I were afraid would happen. I'm not sure you should do too many outings by yourself until people forget about you winning the contest."

Courtney nodded distractedly. She couldn't get over the shock of the encounter. Not at being recognized, though that had been weird, but at the audacity of those men to be so crass and gross to her face. It felt more like the kind of thing you saw on forums from online trolls. What gave them the balls to treat them like that?

"Let's focus on getting ready for tonight, okay?" Olivia said, clearly trying to distract her.

"You were kind of a badass back there."

Olivia shrugged. "After working as an assistant first at Fantasy Island and then as an executive assistant at the Temple, I've learned to have a thick skin. Usually, it's better to just walk away, but sometimes I can't help myself." She paused. "Are you okay?"

Courtney nodded again, then forced herself to take a

deep breath to calm her still fast-beating heart. "I'm fine. I just…hadn't been expecting that. What were you saying about tonight? I thought I had lots of time before I needed to get ready."

Olivia turned her phone around so Courtney could see the text she'd received from Bo.

Bo: Please let Courtney know that we'll be meeting for an early dinner before the show."

"Oh. Shit."

"Exactly. We have a little time to get you ready, but we'll need to move up your appointments with hair and makeup."

"I mean, I could just do it myself…"

This earned Courtney a look. Her immediate thought was how Raife hadn't seemed to mind her DIY style last night, but then Olivia asked, "Do you really want to do it yourself when you could have a team of professionals do it for you?"

That was a fair point. "No." She stifled a sigh and then had to remind herself that she was living most other people's *dreams* right now. A life of luxury, Olivia had called it the other day.

And, she thought with a genuine smile, *I get to see Bo again.* Her heart rate, which had finally begun to slow down, picked right back up at the thought of Bo. She couldn't keep a smile off her face for the rest of the ride back to the Temple.

Olivia left her on her own for half-an-hour so Courtney could get changed into the dress she'd be wearing. It was a blush pink silky affair with spaghetti straps and a low-cut top that draped over her breasts threatening at any second to expose them. It was paired with matching pink heels and made more sophisticated with a slightly darker pink shrug to cover her bare shoulders.

The chime of something arriving in the delivery system made Courtney jump. She opened the small door to find a box inside with a note taped to it.

"What's this?" Courtney murmured to herself. She read the note aloud. "I can't wait to bend you over while you're wearing this. Raife." Her cheeks reddened and she immediately flashed to the memory of his hand covering her mouth as she climaxed.

She didn't have much time, so she ripped the box open as quickly as she could. Inside was a barely-there plaid skirt and a matching, bikini-like crop top. Oddly, there was also a small tie and a pair of black rimmed glasses with no lenses.

Had she not found the card that explained the outfit as a sexy librarian, she would have guessed it was a naughty schoolgirl costume which she wasn't sure she was comfortable with.

Librarian, though...

She smiled. Oh yeah. She could do sexy librarian.

CHAPTER 8

*W*hen she got in the backseat of the SUV, Bo was already in the vehicle waiting for her.

"Courtney, you look..." he paused, taking in her dress while she climbed up into the vehicle. If he was waiting for a nip slip, he'd be waiting a long time. The double-sided tape Olivia had showed Courtney how to use would make sure that didn't happen.

When the driver shut the door behind Courtney, Bo was still staring at her without finishing his sentence.

"I look...what?" She fished, trying not to grin mischievously.

"Like a million bucks," he finally finished, smiling back as the car left the garage and emerged into the evening Vegas sun.

"Hmm. But not a billion, huh?" Courtney was feeling braver after seeing Raife's gift. It was nice to know that someone had enjoyed an encounter with her and wanted more.

The laughter Bo saw dancing in Courtney's eyes sent a

jolt of pleasure through him. It made him happy that she was getting more comfortable in his presence.

"If that dress slips any lower, it might be a billion," he joked but his voice had a slight rasp to it and made Courtney flush a little. Was Bo Ryans really attracted to her?

Maybe this is a real date after all, she thought.

"So, what's the venue for dinner?" She quickly asked to change the subject.

"I thought we'd keep a lower profile tonight. Olivia mentioned that you had a bit of a run-in today with the nastier side of the public."

Courtney's smile vanished as she remembered the man's gross words, and Bo immediately regretted bringing it up as her mood changed.

"I should have listened to you, I guess," she admitted.

"You can't stay cooped up in the Temple forever." At her sideway look, he amended, "Okay, well, yes, I guess you could, but Olivia says you want to see more of the sights while you're here."

"I do. I saw a few things today, but I know there's a lot more to Vegas than just the casinos."

"Like what?" He asked, genuinely curious what would capture her interest.

"Like, there's a whole historical tour about the Vegas mob." Her eyes lit up again, the earlier incident once more forgotten. "And I hear there's a secret underground tunnel that sounds like it would be fun to see. Just...things like that." She trailed off. "I'm sure those sound pretty boring to you since you've lived here for some time now."

"Actually," he said rubbing his chin in that way that Courtney thought made him look sexy, "I've never taken much time to get to know the city."

"Really? There's so much history here!"

"That's right. That's what your degree is in, right? History?"

"How did you know that?"

"It was part of your profile information for the contest." He said, but thought, *And I may have stalked you a little. Okay. A lot.*

"What did you study in college?" Courtney suddenly asked him.

"Mostly economics and business, but I took a little of this and a little of that along the way." He shrugged. "Nothing too exciting."

"What was your favorite class?"

He opened his mouth to give the boring answer he always gave during interviews, but surprised himself when he said instead, "Philosophy, actually."

"Yeah? I wouldn't have guessed that about you. What made you like it?"

He paused. "The subject matter was fascinating of course, but I think it was more the way the professor taught. You could tell she was passionate about it, and it made the class a lot more interesting." Not used to speaking so candidly, Bo started to change the subject but was interrupted.

"Who was your favorite philosopher?"

"Well... Marcus Aurelias was always interesting—"

Courtney barely stopped herself from rolling her eyes but couldn't manage to keep from saying, "An emperor. Of course."

Bo's mouth twitched with the ghost of a smile before he continued answering, "—but Epicurus had a much more profound impact on my way of thinking."

"Isn't Epicurus the guy who was kind of against sex?"

Bo tipped his head a fraction. "He's been quoted as saying, 'Sex never did anyone any good.'"

"So...how can he be your favorite philosopher if he's basically against the very thing you've made money off of? The sex business?"

The grin she received in response to her questions made Courtney wonder what kind of trap she'd just walked into.

"It might look like I'm in the 'sex business' as you put it, but really, I'm in the business of providing people a safe place for pleasure. I know Fantasy Island seems like a twenty-four seven orgy—"

Courtney almost interrupted to tell him that she'd literally seen an advertisement for a Fantasy Island show that was exactly that but decided it would be best to hear him out instead of potentially pushing his buttons at the very beginning of this date.

"—but it only got that way because I allowed it to open up to the public. Initially, it was very much like Pleasure Temple where the focus was pleasure. And, while, yes, pleasure might mean sex for some people, for others, it might mean reading a great book all day with no interruptions. Or a foot massage by a trained masseuse. Keeping Pleasure Temple closed to the outside world by banning social media and requiring nondisclosure agreements from our guests has been one way to allow people to come and actually *not* feel the pressure to participate in sexual encounters."

"Huh. I can see how that makes sense. So, what is it that *does* make Epicurus your go-to guy?" She tried to lighten the mood a little with a smile and was glad that Bo responded with one of his own. She hoped she hadn't offended him by saying he ran a sex business. That hadn't been her intention.

"He prescribed to the idea that we should seek pleasure and avoid pain, but that sometimes pain is unavoidable if our ultimate goal is to achieve a higher level of pleasure. In other words, sometimes we have to make calculated decisions of what pains we'll go through if it means achieving the long-term goals that bring us the most pleasure."

"Hmm." Courtney mulled that over for a moment. Bo appreciated that she was considering this idea rather than dismissing it with a joke or changing the subject. Some of his past girlfriends had done just that when the topic came up or when he wanted to talk philosophy. It wasn't that women he'd dated hadn't been smart, it was that they simply hadn't been interested in this kind of conversation.

Finally, Courtney said, "To a certain extent, I think everyone does that, right? I mean, we work in positions we hate, which is the pain part, just so we can make money to buy the things that bring us pleasure, so I guess he's onto something there." She shifted in her seat and almost laughed as she watched Bo's eyes fight not to jump to the droop of fabric barely covering her breasts. "I guess the real question is, is our outing considered pleasure, or is it part of the pain for your job?"

Bo couldn't keep himself from grinning as Courtney blushed a little at the audacity of her own question. He liked this side of Courtney and only wished he could have a little more time to spend with her. Maybe it would make her even more brash.

"Being with you is all pleasure, Courtney." Bo's deep voice sent a shiver down Courtney's spine. "As for the meetings I cancelled to make tonight happen? Those were absolutely pain."

The ride ended shortly after that and before Courtney knew it, Bo was helping her down from the SUV. For a short, thrilling moment, his hand found the small of her back, but it was gone just as quickly, leaving Courtney wishing he'd touch her again.

He'd chosen a well-known Japanese restaurant with a warm, romantic ambience. When the waiter led them to the table near the waterfall feature, Bo felt he'd made the right choice as Courtney noted how lovely it was.

They made small talk as the waiter took their orders and returned with drinks, but as Courtney sipped plum wine and Bo swirled a whiskey, he asked, "So, your honest opinion now: What do you think of the Temple?"

"I mean, I've only been here for one full day, but so far it's been really nice. There are so many options for, um, encounters in the OCS that it's been interesting to flip through them all. I'm also looking forward to having a personal trainer for the first time." Courtney was proud that she'd managed not to blush when she'd mentioned encounters. "Do you work out on the gym level, or do you have your own private gym on the top floor?" She was genuinely curious. It would be interesting to run into him somewhere in the building. Like, say, the Pleasure level. At this thought she *did* blush.

"I don't usually workout down there because I have a small gym in my apartment, but I do occasionally use the larger gym to run on the track. There's only so much tread-mill a runner can take."

"Oh, you run? Me too! Or, well, I did. I'm planning on taking the opportunity to get back into it while I'm here."

From there they fell into conversation about running and what got them started in the sport. Only occasionally did Courtney remember that she was speaking with a famous billionaire—usually when the waiter returned to check on them or replace their drinks. During the rest of dinner, Courtney continually found herself engaged by his questions. It was refreshing to have someone actually listen to her answers, too.

She began to notice some of his gesturing habits, too. Like that when he wanted to think about an answer, he put his hand to his chin before speaking. Or that, when he could tell how the rest of a story would end, his eyes would grow wide, but he didn't interrupt to say the punchline. She also noticed that he leaned forward a lot, listening attentively when she spoke. Courtney wasn't sure if that was just a good habit formed while trying to win over clients or not. If it was, what was Bo trying to win from her?

For Bo's part, he loved Courtney's witty responses. When they'd first met, he'd been taken with her but had been scared she might be too intimidated by him to be herself. Now he wished they could cut straight to the end of this date so he could get her out of that dress and kiss that spot on her neck she kept self-consciously touching when she told the funny parts of a story. Or the way she struggled but continued trying to use chopsticks to eat the sushi rolls she'd ordered.

Over dessert, Courtney finally found enough courage to broach a subject she'd been thinking about since lunch with Olivia.

"Bo, I kind of feel like Olivia's skills are being wasted on babysitting me. I'm not trying to tell you how to do your job, and, though it's pretty amazing to have a personal assistant like Olivia, I also would feel more comfortable if she had other things to do. As someone who's been a personal assistant, I can't imagine being an executive assistant to you, and then being downgraded to scheduling poker practice sessions and dinner dates for a newb like me."

Rather than being upset that she was poking her nose into his business, he sighed. "I know. I just thought she might need a break, and the contest seemed like the perfect opportunity. I can see that the assignment is chafing her, though. I really don't want to lose her as an employee. I actually had a second, better reason for pulling her off my detail, but it's kind of a surprise for her."

He looked at Courtney more closely as she took a bite of the exquisite tiramisu. His eyes watched her lips wrap around the food, and he had to pry his mind away from where those thoughts led. Instead, he asked, "Are you sure you'd be okay if I assigned her something that took her away from you?"

Courtney shrugged. "I'm sure I can manage on my own. And if I run into something I can't handle on my own, she's only a phone call away."

Bo nodded, and they rolled onto another topic.

After dinner, Courtney found she'd had just enough plum wine that she needed a little of Bo's assistance to manage her heels on the walk to the car waiting for them outside. Bo gladly placed a hand on her hip to keep her upright but was also a little nervous that she'd be able to tell from the heat of his palm how much he wanted to put his hands elsewhere on her body. Or to have his hand on her hips while he pulled her down on top of him.

He shoved those thoughts away as they got in the SUV. After all, there was really no solid indication that she was attracted to him or had feelings for him. Sure, there had been that awkward moment after their dinner in New York when he'd had to suppress an overwhelming desire to kiss her, but had she wanted the same thing? He wasn't sure.

Plus, what if Courtney was just really good at pretending to be interested in him? He'd been in some one-sided relationships before where he'd fallen for the wrong woman. In the last few years, it had been mostly women who were only interested in his bank account.

For some reason, though, he felt like Courtney was different. At least, he really hoped she was.

They made it to the theatre on time and had just managed to take their seats in the private box Bo had reserved as the show started.

Courtney leaned over into Bo's space to whisper, "You 'scrounged up' some seats, did you?" The quirk of her raised eyebrow to indicate the private box made him want to close the short distance between them and kiss her. Had had they been in a more private setting, he might have been brave enough to do it.

Instead, he just gave her his best devilish grin and put his arm on the armrest, hand palm up in an invitation. He saw the surprise in her eyes and for a split second, wondered if he'd made a mistake, but then she smiled and placed her hand in his, keeping her body leaned in his direction.

Was that desire he'd seen in her eyes? He hoped so.

He enjoyed watching her through the show and liked the sound of her laughter and the way she'd periodically turn to him to share a joke. Her hand would occasionally tighten on his during some parts of the play, and he wished again for more privacy. Especially when he'd glimpse the swell of her breasts out of the corner of his eye.

The dress made him think of cotton candy or pink taffy and all he wanted to do was eat her up.

When the show was over and they were back in the car, he found himself once again surprised at how much he enjoyed Courtney's company. And Courtney, in turn, was continually shocked to find that someone like Bo Ryans would find her so intriguing.

As they exited the car, she suddenly realized this might be the end of the date. At the expression on her face, Bo said, "I'll see you to your room if that's okay."

"I would like that," she said, licking her lips self-consciously. She saw the way he watched her tongue and her breath caught in her throat. She covered it with a nervous smile.

When they were in the privacy of the elevator after the doors had closed, Bo said with a voice rough from need, "Courtney, I'd very much like to kiss you. Is that okay?"

She turned, surprised that he was asking and not just going in for the kiss. It was kind of...refreshing. But also, she thought of how Raife had just taken what he'd wanted from her while giving just as good as he got.

"I'd like that."

He leaned down to close the short space between them and, as his lips met hers, she opened herself to him. His kiss, light at first, deepened as she put her hand on his chest. His hand found the small of her back and a white-hot lance of need spiked through her.

Courtney pushed her hips against him, feeling exhilarated. His hand slid further down to squeeze her butt and pulled her harder against him. She could feel his excitement beneath the thin layer of his pants as his hardness pressed against her.

She wanted him but at the back of her mind she also wondered how sex with him after two dates might change their relationship. Would this be a one-time thing? Was he just slumming it with her? She'd seen pictures of some of his past girlfriends in the tabloids. She definitely couldn't compete in the looks department. Hell, some of them had been freakin' models.

Courtney broke away from his kiss to come up for air, both of them breathing heavy now. She wanted to ask him these questions, but she also wasn't sure she wanted to ruin such a great opportunity to have sex with a man she was so clearly attracted to.

The problem, she realized as she gazed up into his questioning eyes, was that she *liked* Bo Ryans. And yes, she also wanted to have her way with him. Or really, for him to have his way with her...but she'd just come out of a long-term relationship and wasn't sure what she wanted at this point.

Not to mention, if they did this, and he suddenly decided he didn't want her at the Temple anymore, she'd have to find a new place to live.

"I'm sorry," Bo said gruffly, one hand still on her butt

while his other hand slid from the back of her neck to gently cup the side of her face.

She leaned into that hand, feeling like a cat looking for more petting. "Don't be, it's just…"

Just what? I want to bang your brains out, but I also kind of want to see where the relationship part of this could go? What relationship? They'd had dinner twice. That was it.

"It's just a little overwhelming." She finished, rather lamely, she thought. Her hand slid from his chest down to his hip. It was a somewhat dangerous move if his small intake of breath was any indication.

He didn't say anything, so she decided to be completely honest.

"I like you, Bo. Like, really like you." Could she sound any more like a freakin' high schooler confessing her love? She forced herself to continue. "More than I thought I would." She tried for a smile. "And I'd *really* like to continue this, this…whatever *this* is." She gestured at the elevator to indicate their passionate kiss. "But I'm not sure what *this* is."

Bo took a deep breath. With it came the scent of Courtney's shampoo, and it was everything he could do not to kiss her again. Instead, he gently rubbed his finger across her jawline. She closed her eyes for a moment, clearly savoring the feel of his hands on her body.

It made him feel better that he wasn't the only one having trouble reeling himself in.

"I get it," Bo finally said. He dropped his hand from her face but only so he could catch her fingers in his as he stepped back to create a little space between them.

Disappointment flashed through Courtney.

So stupid! You could have had sex with Bo Ryans!

The problem was, she didn't feel like it was just going to be sex. Their date and the way he treated her made her feel like it would be more than that. It wouldn't just be sex; it would be making love. A night with Bo would have more weight and meaning behind it than an encounter on the Pleasure level.

What Bo said next proved her right.

He sighed. "You're right. I...like you too, Courtney. God," He grinned and ran his free hand through his hair. "I feel like a schoolboy saying that." He squeezed her hand to emphasize his next words. "I don't usually date guests, and I like to keep relationships exclusive."

"Oh." Courtney wasn't sure how she felt about that. Not that she wanted an open relationship. She'd much prefer an exclusive relationship, too, but...

"I hadn't really planned on jumping into another relation-ship so soon," she blurted out, then turned red, or redder since she was still flushed from the heat of her desire for Bo. "I mean, I literally just broke up with a long-term boyfriend last week."

Bo blew out a breath, then scanned his access card before hitting the button for Courtney's floor. He still held her hand though.

"I'm sorry," she said in a small voice. Had she just blown her chance at a potentially amazing relationship? Or at the very least, really great sex?

He smiled at her and slowly, so that she could push him away if she wanted, he drew her back toward him. His free hand traced her jawline. "Don't be sorry," he whispered and then slowly, oh so slowly that it almost drove Courtney mad with need, he bent down and kissed her even more deeply than before. His hand stayed at her jawline, not pulling her or trying to sway her in any way. His other hand stayed firmly around her own, down at their sides.

It shouldn't have been erotic or sexy, but somehow, his complete openness in letting her choose whether or not to return the kiss made him all the more alluring. Courtney felt drawn into his embrace and found herself once more pressed entirely against him. She felt like she was drinking him in.

If only they could get rid of the pesky material separating them, she could put her mouth on other things. She wanted to see what his skin tasted like under that suit. Was he really that well-built, or were his suits just that well-tailored?

Maybe she'd throw caution to the wind and find out.

They ended up with her pressed against the wall of the elevator. She'd hooked one leg around him and was fumbling with his zipper when the elevator door popped open with a pleasant yet mood-killing tone.

He was the one to pull back this time.

Breath ragged, he put a tiny amount of space between them in order to smooth a hand down her body to fix her now rumpled dress. His hands eventually settled on her hips, effectively pinning her against the elevator wall

What the hell am I doing? He thought

Learning forward, he put his mouth next to her ear and gruffly said, "I want to take you back to your room and make love to you, Courtney. But—"

The word hung in the air for a moment. When Courtney couldn't take it any longer, she finally said, "But?"

He dropped his forehead to her shoulder before blowing out another sigh that sent warm air ghosting down her dress and across her breasts. She drew in a tiny gasp as the sensation of his breath on her skin sent an electric pulse through her. At this point, she'd agree to just about anything.

His hands tightened on her hips, and she thought he might be fighting the urge to hike up her dress and take her right there.

She would have happily let him, and Courtney had a feeling that Bo realized that. Should she be concerned that she was so easily seduced by him? Maybe, but she couldn't seem to care.

When he finally mastered his need, he picked his head back up and whispered, "But I'd want you all for myself, Courtney. Just as I would be only yours while we're together. But I'd want more than sex in an elevator, Courtney. I'd want you as a lover and a confidant. I'd want a real relationship." He sighed again, his breath tickling the fine hairs at her neckline.

"But I don't think you're ready for that, Courtney. And I can't do another casual relationship. It's too difficult."

Now her feelings clamored past the lust. She felt trapped. Not just literally, but figuratively, too. She didn't want to walk right back into another relationship yet. Even if it was with Bo Ryans. Maybe she was being stupid, but being here at the Temple was the opportunity of a lifetime, wasn't it? She'd already learned more about herself and her desires in one night than she had in a long-term relationship.

Bo Ryans might be a billionaire, and she might like him, but she didn't want to jump into a relationship with him just yet if it meant giving up learning more about herself and her own desires.

Courtney closed her eyes so she wouldn't have to look at Bo as she said, "I can't do that right now, Bo. Not yet. I need to learn more about myself first. Be on my own for a little bit."

He pulled away from her, and she opened her eyes just in time to see the hurt in his own eyes before he hid it away. He couldn't quite manage a smile, so he just left his face neutral.

He'd gotten his hopes up too much. He'd really wanted Courtney to be different. And she was. She just wasn't ready for him.

"I had a lovely time tonight, Courtney," his voice was as carefully neutral as he could make it, but his eyes stayed glued to the floor.

Courtney knew a dismissal when she heard it.

She swallowed and pushed away from the wall. "I did, too, Bo." She opened her mouth to say something else, but he stopped her.

"Don't." His eyes snapped up. Anger was easier than feeling like a kicked puppy, so he let it show in his eyes. "I get what you're saying, Courtney. Let's just leave it alone."

His anger made her feel like she'd done something wrong. Why was it the men around her always made her feel that way? All feelings of desire were gone now, replaced by shame and her own slowly building anger though she didn't recognize it as such.

"Fine," she bit out. "Thank you for the nice evening, Bo." With that she waltzed out of the elevator and down the hall.

She almost made it all the way to her room before tears blurred her eyes.

Dot greeted her at the door, meowing her distaste for being left on her own. Courtney picked up the cat and walked them to the bedroom.

What just happened? She asked herself while burying her face in Dot's fur and sinking down onto the bed. *To think, I could have had Bo Ryans in this bed!* But then she kicked herself. *Screw that. I don't need someone who wants me to be exclusive only to him right now. And since when does someone want to be exclusive on the second date?*

More than anything else, Courtney wanted to call Claire and vent about what had happened. It would be nice to get her friend's opinion of the evening. However, she wasn't sure she was allowed to talk about anything since she'd signed that non-disclosure agreement.

She lay in bed for a few minutes and when she finally raised her head, her eyes fell on the drawer where she'd stowed her gift from Raife.

Perhaps she'd find some other way to vent her frustration. The idea put a smile on her face, so she popped off the bed, further annoying Dot, and yanked open one of the bureau drawers.

"I know someone who will play with me tonight," she said and sent Raife a message she hoped would entice him to come play before carrying the fun new outfit to the bathroom to change.

* * *

LIKE IN THEIR PREVIOUS ENCOUNTER, Courtney reached the assigned room before Raife. She was appropriately dressed in her sexy librarian outfit for the room she now stood in that was lined with full bookshelves that gave off that alluring scent of old books. Unfortunately, Courtney's jangling nerves kept her from browsing the shelves. She wanted to be ready when Raife arrived.

A large, sturdy desk sat in the center of the room with an old-school wooden chair that had leather covered padding. On the desk was a stack of books and a name plate stating that the desk belonged to the Head Librarian. Steel bolts were placed in pairs all over the desk.

Rather than feel nervous at the sight of the bolts, Courtney found that they gave her a little thrill.

The better to tie you down with, my dear, Courtney thought then clapped a hand over her mouth to stifle a giggle.

The only other piece of furniture in the room was a sort of fainting couch. She wasn't sure it belonged in a library, but she could see how the soft leather would make for a more pleasant sexual encounter than the desk might.

It wasn't what she had in mind though.

Her hands nervously brushed her bare thighs as she approached the desk. The plaid skirt was so short, it was a wonder everything wasn't hanging out. It was cool in the room, so her nipples were already hard under her top. Or maybe that was just from anticipation.

She'd even worn the silly glasses to complete the outfit. She'd decided that if she was going to do this, she might as well go all in.

The door opened behind her. She turned and caught her breath. Just the very sight of Raife, shirtless and wearing those same leather pants turned her on.

Or maybe it was the mask.

Or the silk ties in his hands.

He smiled, and she could hardly believe the amount of pure lust his smile inspired in her. It somehow made her feel watery and brave all at the same time.

She backed up and scooted her butt up onto the edge of the desk as he crossed the space between.

Placing her hands to either side of her and leaning back a bit, she snapped, "You're late, young man," It was her best tart librarian voice, "and I've heard that you've been being too loud."

He'd closed the distance between them. When he reached her, he spread her legs apart by pushing his hips between them. His mouth found hers at the same time as his hand gripped her back and scooted her forward against him.

He was already rock solid and raring to go.

Yum.

Before she could wonder what his plans were this time, his mouth left hers and trailed down her throat, across her chest to her left breast. He nosed the material out of the way and let his tongue caress her nipple, sending a jolt to her groin. She bucked forward into him, hoping he'd realize she wanted him to pull off her thong and take her like this. Or maybe spin her around and take her from behind like before.

He had other plans though. His hand took the place of his mouth, squeezing her breast just on the edge of being painful, then releasing. She closed her eyes as he leaned her further back on the desk, his body weight pressing her down. Then his hands found hers, and before she realized it, he'd tied them overhead and anchored them to the desk.

Damn. This guy is experienced.

She jerked her hands against the silk ties and found them quite solid. The feeling of being utterly at his mercy was... exhilarating. What would he do next?

"Open your eyes," he demanded.

She complied and watched him run his hands deliciously from her arms down her sides, over the side swell of her breasts, and down to her waist. Here he pulled her down the desk a little as he pushed himself harder against her. She gasped and lifted toward him in an automatic reaction.

Did he know he'd found a sweet spot there?

His grin told her yes.

His hands left her waist, traveled down her thighs, first smoothing down the skirt, then moved back up underneath the flimsy material. He pulled her thong off and dropped it to the floor.

Then he yanked up her skirt and, while keeping his eyes glued to hers, lowered his head to put his tongue on that sweet spot as if claiming it for himself. Slowly, achingly slowly, he moved his tongue up and down.

"*Yes,*" she moaned, not wanting him to stop.

He then took her entirely in his mouth and sucked.

Electricity zapped through her and her whole body went rigid, her mind focused solely on the sensation between her legs. When he stopped sucking, his tongue slid inside her. She gasped in pleasure and snapped her eyes closed in surprise.

He suddenly stopped and pulled back. "Open your eyes, Courtney. I want you to watch."

The command was almost enough to snap her out of the

scene. But this was a part of it, right? This was why she'd left her kink level at a two in the system.

And, truth be told, she kind of liked the whole being dominated thing.

"Your message said you wanted me to make you beg for more. I can do that," Raife practically purred. He darted his tongue forward against that sweet spot again, and she sucked in air at the feeling and lifted her hips, splaying her legs wider.

"Open. Your. Eyes," he demanded again.

She felt him shift his body and followed his command—mostly to see what he was doing. She found him looking down at her, his mouth set in a stern line.

"Good. Very good, Courtney." His stern countenance was replaced with a look of devilish mischief that sent a little thrill of anticipation through her.

What would he do next?

His fingers dipped under her skirt and touched that sweet spot, very gently rubbing. Almost teasing. His eyes stayed locked on hers, and she couldn't help but wiggle and move her hips along with his fingers, hoping for more. She began to ache with need, wanting him to keep going while at the same time, hoping he'd fill her with himself again.

Still keeping his eyes on her, he yanked his leather pants down just enough to clear his erect penis. He stopped pleasuring her just long enough to grip her hips and jerk her closer to him, moving her bottom right to the edge of the desk and stretching her arms taunt against the silk bonds.

In one swift move he thrust into her, filling her up and making her moan. At the same time, he found his way back to gently stimulating her with his fingers as he pulled back and slowly pushed into her again. She struggled to keep her eyes open as his own bore into hers and he slowly pulled out of her.

"Do you like this, Courtney. Do you want more?"

When she didn't answer right away, he stopped moving his fingers against her.

A part of her cried out not to stop.

"Yes! Yes. I do," she panted. "I want more."

His fingers found her again and this time he slipped his other hand under her butt, tipping her hips at a slightly different angle. Then, unexpectedly, he shoved himself hard inside her. She gasped and wrapped her legs around his waist. Even with her eyes open, it was easy to imagine that the masked Raife was really Bo, taking her body however he wanted to.

She moaned to the gentle working of his fingers and the rhythmic thrust of him sliding in and out of her. Pressure began to build within her, threatening to explode.

Just when she thought she would burst, he reached up and pinched her nipple between his fingers, not hard, but enough to cause a sweet note of pain to slip through the pleasure. She cried out in surprise, but what sent her over the edge was the look of total domination in Raife's eyes as he pushed himself inside her. Hard.

It was the crack in the dam that she'd needed. The pressure spilled over, and she tipped her head back as waves of pleasure racked her body and carried her mind away for a few seconds. Raife came a few seconds after that, silently shuddering on top of her.

When she found herself again, she was still breathing heavy. Her hands had been untied. She sat up just in time to see Raife disappear through the door leaving her alone once again.

How did Raife escape so efficiently with her barely even noticing? She was hardly mad at him. It was kind of a relief to not feel obligated to continue having sex after already orgasming once. She'd never been a woman who could have more than one orgasm a night.

Then again, here at the Temple, she was learning all kinds of new things about herself.

Namely, that she didn't know that much about what she liked in the first place.

It's time to be bold and make some new self-discoveries, she thought as she made her way back up to her room. It was the same thought she had as she fell asleep that night, wondering what pushing her kink up to a level three would be like.

Time to be bold.

CHAPTER 9

*C*ourtney didn't see Bo again for two weeks though she continued to have regular encounters with Raife. Her days took on a rhythm filled with personal interests and activities that she hadn't been able to do while working in New York. She fell into a routine of working out with the Temple's personal trainer, eating breakfast by herself after showering, then finding something to do in the apartment like read or binge TV before having lunch in the staff area with Olivia or one of the other staff members she'd gotten to know.

In the afternoons, Courtney found that the best thing to do was to schedule official tours in the city or guided hikes out in the desert.

During her outings, she liked to take pictures and post them to her social media which she kept under a fake name. It was a holdover from not wanting to accidentally post something inappropriate that would get her fired from her job. She'd never really had the time to post stuff before, and it was fun to try different things with camera filters, stickers, and short video clips. Before long, she began to start attracting more followers.

She tried to make it a point to leave the Temple at least three or four times a week if she could help it, just to remind herself of the real world. And on the days that she wasn't out sightseeing, she was learning how to be better at poker, blackjack, and craps. Blackjack was her favorite out of the three, but she hadn't yet tried it in a real casino by herself. She wasn't sure she wanted a repeat of the ugly interaction she and Olivia had experienced at the food court.

Unless Courtney had something else scheduled, lunch was the only time she and Olivia connected in person during the day. True to his word, Bo found other projects for Olivia to work on rather than just babysitting Courtney all the time. She and Olivia had agreed to have lunch each day, though, so that Courtney could catch Olivia up on how things were going since Olivia was still technically assigned to assist Courtney.

Today, the two decided to sit out on the balcony reserved for staff while they ate a lunch of roast chicken and vegetables drizzled with truffle oil. Courtney was already starting to see a difference in her figure from working out and eating healthy. She still indulged in the occasional dessert and sugary mixed drink but was still losing weight and gaining muscle. She thought part of it was due to being so happy lately.

Not to mention her extra workouts in the evening with Raife.

She'd left her kink at a level two and so far, she didn't feel like things were too far out of her comfort zone. In all honesty, she'd been toying with going up another level...but that wasn't a conversation for today.

"So, I've been thinking about how to fill some of my time in the afternoons while I'm here," Courtney said, running a piece of broccoli around her plate to soak up more truffle oil.

"Oh? Bored of the sights already?"

Olivia had started feeling more and more like a friend than a staff member. It wasn't just because Courtney couldn't talk to anyone else because of the nondisclosure agreement. Part of their budding friendship was due to the fact that they'd both been assistants to some pretty narcissistic people. It was fun swapping stories.

"No," Courtney smiled across the table, "but I bet the tour guides will get sick of me after a while. I'm already on a first-name basis with most of them."

"You could always schedule some more sessions with Raife." A wicked grin lit up Olivia's face.

"I think I like keeping that kind of thing relegated to the evenings. Actually, I was thinking of taking some classes. I mean, I have some money to use, and what better time to knock out online classes than while I have free room and board?"

"That's...not a bad idea." Olivia said and placed her fork thoughtfully down on her plate. "Any particular areas of study in mind yet?"

"I thought about a master's degree but that would take at least two years, and I'm only here for three months, so I was thinking about pursuing certifications in social media management. I mean, I've built up quite a few followers on my own social media and have learned a ton about when to post and how to use schedulers and other tools like that. It's been kind of fun, to be honest, and I think it would be interesting to learn how to apply that kind of stuff to marketing for businesses."

Olivia nodded. She'd been following Courtney's social media account, not just to ensure she didn't break the NDA, but also because Courtney had a knack for seeing things that other people didn't and posting them.

"I think that's a great idea, Courtney! There's always a demand for social media managers for large and small businesses. You could do it from anywhere you wanted, too."

"That's what I was thinking, too." Courtney looked down at her plate. "I'm not sure I want to go back to New York after my time here is up."

Olivia waited for Courtney to elaborate and when she didn't, Olivia decided to push a little. "Because you're bored of New York, or because you don't want to deal with Daniel?"

Courtney's head jerked up. Was she really so transparent?

Olivia put down her fork and sighed. "Look, I know this has been a weird experience for you—a good experience," she amended, "but still weird. I know it's annoying not to be able to really talk to anyone about your experiences here because of the NDA, and it's nice that you feel comfortable talking to me—"

Here she paused and Courtney wondered if this was when Olivia would finally come out and say that this was strictly business and that they weren't friends.

"—and honestly, I know I started out as your assistant, so this was more of a business relationship, but I hope you know that I consider you a friend now."

Courtney couldn't help the smile that lit up her face. "Really? I mean, I kind of felt like we were becoming friends, too, but I didn't want you to feel like you *had* to be my friend for your job, you know?"

"I do, but I do feel like we're friends. And that's how I'm telling you this—as a friend: Don't go back to New York unless you have to. Three months might seem like a long time to be away, but when you go back to a place where you were miserable, it's too easy to fall back into old habits and find yourself back down that hole of misery. You know?"

Courtney nodded.

"Good. Now, talk to Olivia the assistant. Tell me more about this social media thing. Do you need anything for it? Like a laptop or help getting into a program?

Courtney couldn't help but grin as she saw Olivia slip into her assistant persona.

"I'm already ahead of you. I ordered a laptop last night when I finally decided to apply for an online academy."

Right after coming back from having mind-blowing sex with Raife in a faux wood cabin on a bear skin rug in front of a roaring fire. It sounded romantic, but Raife's mask had made it seem somehow dangerous. That, and he'd taken her from behind while she was on all fours after forcing her to the ground.

Courtney had to suppress a shiver at the memory. There was something about having zero control in the bedroom that she found really turned her on. And yet, during the day, it made her want to take more control over her life and start making decisions on what she wanted to do next.

"I'll get a certificate that I can put on my resume at the end of the training," she added.

"When do you start the program?"

"As soon as I get the laptop. It's online and self-paced, so I can really do it anytime."

"Better leave your nights open, though," Olivia joked. As they laughed, Courtney realized that if Olivia had made that joke only a week ago, Courtney would have blushed. Now she was kind of proud of her sexual encounters.

When their laughter died down, Olivia added, "Actually, there's something else I wanted to talk to you about while I have my assistant hat on. Bo wanted to know if you'd like to accompany him to a sort of gambling charity event at one of the local casinos. He said to let you know that he'd pay for the cover charge and not to argue about it."

"What?" Courtney asked, her surprise and confusion plainly showing. She hadn't shared any of the details about her and Bo's date with Olivia because she hadn't been sure Olivia would want to hear about her boss's personal life like that.

"Actually, um, I kind of thought Bo wasn't interested in seeing me anymore."

Olivia's eyebrows shot to her forehead. "What made you think that?"

"I know you probably don't need to hear this since Bo is your boss and no one needs that kind of drama, but..." and then Courtney gave the cliff notes version of her conversation with Bo in the elevator. When she finished, she couldn't help but add, "So, I'm not really sure why he'd want to see me again."

Olivia stayed quiet while Courtney relayed the conversation, then sat in thought for a moment afterwards before saying, "I don't think Bo was as put off by what you talked about in the elevator as you think. I hadn't really thought about it, but when I do connect with him for other projects, he almost always asks how you're doing and if you're enjoying yourself. It's nothing invasive," she quickly added. "What you tell me about your experiences here as a friend stays between us, but I do let him know, in general, how you're doing."

If he didn't want to have a relationship that was nonexclusive, and she'd told him she wasn't ready for that, why was he pushing for another date-like outing and asking after her?

"Maybe I'm reading too much into the invite?"

Olivia opened her mouth, then clamped it shut again, clearly holding something back.

"What? Spill it, Olivia. What am I missing here? Does he just need someone to go to the event with him?"

After a brief hesitation during which Olivia weighed whether or not she should be giving her boss's personal information away, she decided that Courtney deserved to be prepared.

"Usually, Bo goes to these things by himself. The last time he really dated anyone was Kitty Summers, and I'm sure you know how that turned out."

Courtney shook her head. "I don't keep up with that kind of tabloid stuff. What happened?"

Olivia blew out a sigh and leaned in while keeping her voice somewhat lowered. "Kitty Summers was a walking disaster in the disguise of a devoted and loving girlfriend. She pulled the wool over all our eyes, but most of all Bo's. Hell, we're pretty sure he would have proposed just to make her happy, then the shit hit the fan and Kitty showed us her real face. But Diana—"

"Dragon-lady Diana?" Courtney interrupted in an equally low voice.

"Yes, that Diana, but don't say that where others can hear you. Anyway, Diana never liked her. She was the one who discovered that Kitty was just cozying up to Bo so she could get secrets about Pleasure Temple and sell them to the highest bidder, which turned out to be Ace Lockhart. Of course, by then, it was too late to do anything about it."

"Wait, isn't that the guy who started Carnal Temptations? Oh!" Though Courtney kept up in general with national and world news, she'd never been one for news based around business or entertainment figures.

However, there was one story that had hit the national news about Lockhart Industries getting sued by Bo Ryans. It had been a big deal but then died out when the lawsuit didn't go anywhere, and honestly, it probably would have been just a blip on the radar—except for the sex tape.

"Wait, is Kitty the woman in the sex tape with Bo?"

Olivia nodded. "That's her."

The video had been of a somewhat grainy quality, but it had clearly been Bo in the video having very energetic and slightly kinky sex with a woman who was mostly blocked by Bo's body. The woman had been blindfolded with her hands tied to something in the ceiling. Bo had taken her almost violently from behind and the only sound in the tape was Bo saying, "Is this want you want?" While he repeatedly thrust into her.

When Courtney had first seen the video, it had definitely felt a little disturbing, but she also remembered reading that the woman in the video had said it was consensual. Courtney had written it off after that. What other people did in the bedroom was not her business as long as both parties were okay with it, but others hadn't seen things that way. It had become kind of a smear campaign against Bo and Pleasure Temple.

Now, after experiencing several encounters at the Temple, Courtney thought it might be fun to be in Kitty's place.

After the video hit the internet, the lawsuit disappeared shortly after.

"So, what does Kitty have to do with Bo asking me to this event?"

"Word is that she's going to be there…as Ace Lockhart's date."

"Oh." Did Bo just want her as arm candy to make Kitty jealous? It seemed unlikely. Courtney might feel good about herself and her body now, but she still wasn't a super model. Bo would be better off asking one of his former girlfriends to go with him.

She pushed these thoughts away though and instead said, "That sucks. Why does Bo even plan to attend then? Can't he just donate and skip it?"

Olivia sighed. "This is Bo we're talking about here. He's gone to this event every year. If he doesn't go the one year that Lockhart does, it's like giving up more territory to the man."

Courtney rolled her eyes. "That's so stupid."

"I couldn't agree more. But it doesn't change Bo's mind. He'll still go."

Playing with her water glass, Courtney looked away from Olivia and decided to voice her thoughts from earlier. "Maybe he should pick someone who would, I dunno, make better arm candy?" Now she looked up. "Isn't there some model he could take who would do a better job at making Kitty jealous? That's the point after all, right?"

"Yes and no. You're looking at it from the wrong angle. Bo broke up with Kitty because she's the one who leaked that tape. Kitty is going with Ace Lockhart to make Bo jealous. Kitty still wants to be with Bo. The day he kicked her out of the Temple?" Olivia leaned back and whistled. "Let's just say, I'm glad I was busy elsewhere. I heard it was quite the shit show, though. Tears, screaming, broken glass—the works. The thing is, I'm not sure Kitty really ever had feelings for Bo, though. She definitely liked the status that being Bo's girlfriend gave her. But she didn't realize what she was losing until it was gone."

"I mean, she probably shouldn't have leaked the tape then, right?"

Olivia shrugged. "I think Kitty is one of those women who craves attention and power. And by making and leaking that tape, which I'm pretty sure was a suggestion from Ace Lockhart, she thought she'd get both. But Bo doesn't play those kinds of games, and once she realized how her actions affected her relationship with Bo and as a result, her lifestyle, only then was she sorry. Not for what she did to Bo, but for what she'd pissed away."

"Damn." It all Courtney could think to say about such an underhanded play for attention.

Olivia began gathering her empty dishes onto her tray, and Courtney did the same before they both stood and headed for the dish return area.

"Okay." Courtney said as they walked, "But that still doesn't explain why Bo would want to take me to the event."

Olivia turned to catch Courtney's eyes. "You really don't pay attention to any of the tabloids, do you?"

"No. Should I?" Courtney's stomach suddenly clenched.

"Courtney," Olivia blew out a sigh of exasperation. "Pictures of you and Bo are plastered all over them like you're trying to infiltrate the royal family or something."

"What?" A spike of fear hit her.

"Bo hasn't really dated anyone since Kitty. So, when the paparazzi saw him out with you—twice—they decided you must be his new girlfriend."

"Okay. That's…that's not so bad, right? I mean, I'm *not*, but still…"

"Courtney," Olivia sounded like she was struggling not to chide Courtney for her naivety. "They're saying that you didn't 'win' the contest, but that Bo picked you, specifically. So that he could take you here…to be his sex toy."

"What?! That's bullshit, Olivia!"

"Shhh," Olivia gestured for Courtney to calm down, then led her into an alcove that held a small bench for a slightly more private conversation. "I know that, and you know that…but to the rest of the world?" She shrugged. "I mean, you're not the only person who won the contest, but you don't see Bo taking Galin Hammer to dinner or the theatre just because he's the other contest winner, do you?"

Courtney made a noise of protest and plopped down onto the bench. She couldn't disagree with Olivia's statement. And it wasn't like the tabloids were entirely wrong. Bo was interested in her, but not as a sex toy, for heaven's sake.

"I'm sorry," Olivia said. "I thought you knew. It's why I was concerned about you going out by yourself. I thought the paparazzi would follow you or that the public would heckle you like that guy at the food court."

"I didn't know." Courtney tried to keep the anger from her voice and failed. "I'm sorry. I'm not mad at you. I just...I thought I could have three months here, get the social media certificate, then get an entry level job somewhere to kind of start over, you know? But now," she gestured at the window across the hall from them as if to take in the outside world, "how the hell am I supposed to have any semblance of a normal life if the tabloids keep plastering my face everywhere? How will I know that the next job I get won't be because some guy thinks I'll help him get his rocks off?"

Olivia sat down on the bench next to Courtney. "I'm sorry. I really am. There's not much we can do about the tabloids. Any kind of official statement of denial is seen as a sort of admission of guilt." She put a hand on Courtney's shoulder. "But we might be able to help on the job front. Remember that Bo has holdings all over the world. I'm sure one of them could use someone in their marketing department to help build up their social media presence. Or whatever you decide to do next."

"Don't you think that will just confirm their theories? It would almost be worse because they'd say I got the job because I'm sleeping with Bo—which I'm not." Courtney quickly clarified then stood. "I need to go think about this, I guess."

"I understand. But don't forget to let me know if you plan to go with Bo to the charity event." Before Courtney could argue, Olivia held up a placating hand. "I know, I know. But honestly, going with him won't make things any worse. The tabloids have already decided what the story is on you. Avoiding Bo isn't going to change that."

Courtney nodded and made an excuse to leave, but as she made her way back up to her suite, she thought that another reason for not accepting Bo's invitation to the event was that she didn't want him to think she was leading him on. She felt like she was only scratching the surface of learning what she liked and what she didn't like. She wasn't ready to be exclusive and potentially cut off this sudden self-discovery.

Hell, she'd actually been considering branching out even from Raife and having an encounter with someone new. Now that her interests and desires were public, she'd had several other invitations that she'd turned down. Now Courtney wondered if some of those invites had been due to her being in the papers.

Gah.

It felt like she'd have to start questioning *everything* now.

Back in her suite, she picked up Dot from where she had been sleeping in a chair and then sat down with the cat on her lap.

After a moment of prickly annoyance at having been disturbed, Dot settled onto Courtney's lap and began to purr. Courtney stroked her soft cheek.

She turned on the TV and tried to forget about what Olivia had told her, but it was no good. Annoyed with herself but unable to escape the needle of curiosity poking at her brain, she stood and put Dot back on the chair and picked up the tablet before dropping cross-legged onto the couch.

The cat sniffed in disdain before standing to stretch and stare at Courtney in reproach. Then she jumped off the chair and stalked into the bedroom so as not to be disturbed.

"Sorry, Dot," Courtney murmured, "I've gotta know."

She pulled up the first tabloid she could think of and caught her breath.

At the very top of the page was a picture of her and Bo from their second dinner date. It was the moment that Bo had put his hand on her waist to steady her on their way to the car before the show. His hand was circled in bright red ink next to the headline, "Is Bo Ryans Getting Too Handsy with the Pleasure Temple Contest Winner?"

"Shit," Courtney breathed.

She scrolled down to see another picture of Bo as he caught her when she'd stumbled out of the SUV on their first date. Further down was an older picture of Bo and a different woman with large print below shouting, "Is Bo Really Over Kitty?"

The woman was a beautiful petite blond with perfect features, perfect makeup, and the perfect figure.

"Ugh. This is such garbage." Courtney had to stop herself from throwing the tablet across the room.

She'd seen ridiculous tabloids before, usually sitting at the beginning of the supermarket checkout lanes. They'd seemed laughable then. Of course, she'd never thought she'd be gracing their covers. Other people clearly read them and might believe their lies.

"Oh no," she moaned as she realized she knew exactly who read that kind of crap.

She called her mother, dread sitting in her stomach as it rang through. Finally, her mom picked up.

"I see you've decided you have a mother after all, huh?"

"I'm sorry, Mom. I've just been…busy." Her eyes flicked to the tablet, and she realized she'd given her mother just the opening she needed.

"Busy, huh? Busy getting into bed with Bo Ryans, I see."

"Mom!"

"What? I'm not blind you know. I've seen the papers."

"Those stories aren't really real, Mom. You know that."

"So, you and Bo aren't dating? Because those pictures of you two together look real enough."

"No, Mom, it's…agh." Courtney dropped her head against the back of the couch and closed her eyes. "We're not *dating*-dating. We just went out a few times. That's all."

"Are you sure?"

"I mean, he'd like it to be more—"

"But you don't?"

"It's complicated, Mom. I just broke up with Daniel. And, c'mon, why would Bo Ryans be interested in someone like me?"

There was a moment of silence before her mom said, "If he's not interested, why would he want more than a just a few dates? And what has you saying no to that?"

"Well, for starters," Courtney spluttered, "my face is splattered all over the tabloids! I don't want that." It wasn't the real reason, but it was what she was currently pissed about. Plus, should she tell her mother that she was getting bent over by Raife almost every night and reaching the pinnacle of orgasms at his hands? And tongue…and other things.

"Oh, give me a break, Courtney. You wanted to try something new, and you went to Vegas. Now that new thing is scaring you, so you're backing down."

"N-no, that's not it."

"Then what is it?"

Courtney sighed. She didn't want her mother to think she was sex-crazy or a nymphomaniac, but she also didn't want to lie to her. "He wants to be exclusive. And if I'd met him at any other time in my life, I would be totally fine with that! But this is my chance to kind of find out who I am. I don't want to just jump from one guy to another. I want to be on my own for a bit."

"Hmm."

Courtney couldn't tell if her mother was judging her or agreeing with her, so she added, "He invited me out again to something more public. I don't know if I should say yes. I already told him I didn't want to be exclusive, but he invited me anyways. What do you think I should do, Mom? If I go, I'll just create more fuel for the tabloids."

There was another silence, and then her mom asked, "Do you like being with him?"

Courtney sighed again. She thought of Bo's warm smile and how he genuinely seemed to listen to what she said. She'd enjoyed their conversations and there was definitely a spark between them. It would be fun to get to know him more...but not if it meant losing her current independence.

"Yes," Courtney finally said in a tone filled with self-disgust. "I do."

"Then if he knows you don't want to be exclusive and he invited you out again anyways, then it's his fault if he gets hurt. He's a big boy. I think he can take it." She chuckled. "Besides, I'm getting sick of seeing the same pictures of you and him over and over in the papers. Let's give them something new to post for a change."

Courtney couldn't help the choked laugh that escaped her throat. They spoke a bit longer, catching up. Her mom was all for Courtney pursuing training in social media management and thought it was a good idea to pursue a new career at the end of the three months.

"It'll fly by, Courtney," her mom said just before they got off the call. "Enjoy it while you can."

When Courtney hung up, she blew out a breath in resolve, then picked up the tablet to message Olivia.

Courtney: Looks like I'm going to the ball.

Olivia's response was almost immediate: Charity Event. I'll godmother-up some hair and make-up artists. It's time for a touch up on your nails, too. I'll book you an appointment at the spa for tomorrow. I recommend the white cock-tail dress or the black and white diamond one.

Courtney looked down at her fingernails and shrugged. She hadn't noticed that the polish on them had become quite chipped in spots. She'd never really been a nail polish kind of gal after high school. Now it seemed to be some kind of necessary evil while she was here at the Temple.

Ah well, she knew she shouldn't complain. She just didn't want to get too used to all the pampering. It would only make it all the more difficult to go back to the real world when this was all over.

CHAPTER 10

*C*ourtney spent most of the next day at the spa. She started with a mud bath, then an amazing massage, followed by a not so amazing waxing session. It helped that when she arrived for the waxing torture, the technologist handed her a mimosa as soon as she walked in and said, "For the pain."

That was followed by an eyebrow shaping session, then a pedicure, and finally a manicure. By that time, she was ready for a break and escaped to the staff area for a late lunch.

She'd missed her window to have lunch with Olivia, so she sat alone, enjoying a slice of a personal cheese, basil, and mushroom pizza while she read articles on her phone about how to break into social media management. Pursuing her interest in social media felt like the right move, but she was nervous that she wouldn't be able to get a job without a degree in marketing.

She still had a little over seven thousand dollars left from her contest winnings even after purchasing the laptop, paying for the online academy, and buying a few clothes to restock her basic wardrobe, but she wanted to hold enough cash back to use as a down payment wherever she ended up moving. Not to mention she'd need to furnish a new apartment. There were also the taxes she'd have to pay for the contest winnings and all those dresses and accessories. It was hard to give up having that safety net in her bank account, but the reality was that though the money was there now, it was mostly already spent.

As she pondered her best path forward, a sudden voice behind Courtney startled her, making her jump half out of her chair.

"Courtney! There you are!" William, Olivia's assistant, strolled up to her, all smiles.

Courtney was unable to dredge up a return smile when she saw the person trailing behind him, looking around like he was at a theme park and was taking in the sights.

"Look who I found in the reception area!" William said. When he saw Courtney's clear surprise and, what she hoped wasn't too much annoyance, he paused. "This *is* your boyfriend, isn't it? He said he was." The assistant looked between Courtney and Daniel, suddenly unsure.

"He *was* my boyfriend. We're just...friends now, William."

"Oh. Uh…" He trailed off, clearly not sure how to fix the situation.

"I've got it from here, William," Courtney said with the ghost of a smile. "Thanks."

He gave her a half-reassured smile in return, then retreated like he couldn't get away fast enough.

"Daniel. What are you doing here?"

He stepped forward as if to hug her, but she put out a hand to stop him. "I told him we're friends so that he wouldn't feel bad for letting you in here, but you and I both know that we're not. So? What are you doing here?" She bit off the last words then dropped her unfinished pizza onto the plate.

He backed off with a frown but took the liberty of taking a seat across from her.

"I missed you, babe."

"Babe? Since when do you call me that?" She stopped, realized she was getting sidetracked, and waved away her own question. "What are you really doing here, Daniel?"

"I told you. I missed you, Courtney. I really did. I wanted to come out here to apologize. I realize now that I shouldn't have asked you not to come here. This place is…great," he breathed, looking around in awe.

But as Courtney watched him, she realized he wasn't looking at the building, he was looking at the people. Specifically at a group of beautiful women who were eating together a few tables over. Courtney recognized one of them as a staff member from the Pleasure level. The woman, Annie, looked up and smiled at them. Courtney smiled back, then looked at Daniel.

"Hey. Earth to Daniel."

His eyes snapped back to her. The moment they did, Courtney got a weird feeling. She didn't buy for a minute that Daniel missed her. He'd already tried that spiel over the phone. It seemed totally unlike him to fly all the way out to Vegas just to repeat their conversation. Courtney narrowed her eyes as she began to wonder if Daniel was here of his own accord.

"Sorry, I was just distracted," he said, then quickly covered up his lapse of attention by saying, "Listen, can we go somewhere more private? I'd like to be able to talk to you without a crowd around. You've got a room here, right?"

"You know I do, Daniel. And no," she sat back, crossing her arms over her chest. "We can stay right here and chat."

Daniel leaned forward. "Courtney, come on. Don't be like

that. Don't you trust me anymore? Or are you afraid that if we're alone you'll maybe realize how much you missed me?" His grin was an attempt to get her to smile, but she wasn't taking the bait.

"I've honestly got things to do, Daniel. So, tell me why you're here or leave."

The fake smile fell from his face, and he sat back with a huff.

"I told you, Courtney. I'm here to see you. God! Am I not allowed to miss you now? You've been gone for over two weeks! I wanted to see you and talk to you. You look really great, you know? This place has done you a lot of good."

Courtney watched him for a moment. Could he really actually have started to miss her? Once upon a time she would have believed him. After all, they'd been happy once, hadn't they? And maybe he'd been happy the whole time, and it was Courtney who had been the one to lose interest.

A tiny part of her started to feel bad for leaving, and then she saw his eyes flick to the table of beautiful women again. Her distrust returned.

She put her arms on the table. "No. You're not just here to talk to me. You're here for something else, though I honestly don't know what it is you think you'll get from me. You know I'm not rich. You know my being here is just a short-term thing. So, what is it that you're really here for, Daniel?"

She lifted an eyebrow as he opened his mouth to lie. She knew his tells, and the way he was bouncing one of his legs under the table told Courtney all she needed to know about what was about to come out of his mouth.

"Don't lie to me, Daniel," she said, cutting him off before the lie crossed his lips. "Why are you here?"

"Courtney, I really, truly did miss you," he leaned forward again, and this time reached out to place his hand on her arm. "Please believe me."

Lie. Lie. Lie. It was written all over his body.

How had she ever stayed with a jerk like this?

She pulled her arm away and stood, gathering her tray with the half-eaten pizza. "I have to go, Daniel. I have an appointment to get to."

He stood as well, but his face was screwed down in anger now. "Oh, I'm *sorry*. Am I keeping you from your new boyfriend? That didn't take long, did it? Did you even wait until you got here to hop into bed with him, or did he bang you while you were still back in New York?"

It was such a quick switch of emotion that the heat of his response surprised Courtney into silence. When she recovered, she quietly said, "I have to go," then turned to make her way over to the dish return section.

He grabbed her arm and jerked her back to him. The move caused the tray to slip from her hand, sending the pizza plate clattering loudly to the floor. A quick glance told Courtney that everyone was watching them now. She couldn't help the blush spreading across her face.

Daniel had never touched her in violence before, but now his face twisted in an ugly kind of anger that made her think he wanted to do more than crush her arm.

"I *said* I need to talk to you in *private*, Courtney." His eyes bore into hers, demanding that she listen and follow his command. Suddenly, he dropped her arm and stepped back a pace, slipping a smile back into place so quickly Courtney almost thought she'd imagined the threat of violence she'd seen in his eyes. "Look, let's just go to your room and talk, okay?"

Did he really think she was going be alone with him after that little outburst?

"No," she said quietly, then more forcefully. "No, Daniel. I'm not going anywhere with you. Go home. Go back to New York. We're done. We've been done. I don't know why you came all the way out here. There's nothing left to talk about."

"Courtney—"

"I think the lady asked you to leave."

The familiar voice felt like a life raft on an unexpectedly turbulent sea. Courtney didn't have to look behind her to know that Bo was a solid wall at her back. She had to fight the unexpected pull to back into him for protection.

"Oh wow, Bo Ryans!" Daniel practically chortled. Courtney was having trouble understanding how Daniel could go from such anger at Bo for dating Courtney to suddenly fangirling all over him. "It's so great to meet you!"

Courtney took the opportunity to step to the side so that she could see both men at the same time. Bo wore a silvery-grey suit that lent him an even more powerful air. Normally, her eyes might have lingered on him longer, but the air still had an edge of violence to it with Daniel around.

"You must be Daniel, I presume. Courtney's…"

"Ex-boyfriend," Courtney quickly filled in before Daniel could say otherwise, "and he was just leaving."

"Oh, come on, Courtney," Daniel practically whined, "I just got here."

She turned to him, flailing for how to tell him to leave again before finally realizing that the simple truth was the best option. "I have things to do today, Daniel. Please don't drop in unexpected again." She returned to the table and pulled some napkins from the holder there, then picked up the overturned pizza and began to wipe the splattered sauce from the floor.

"Won't you at least see me out?" Daniel tried in a last-ditch effort, then pissed away any real chance with Courtney by adding, "Why are you cleaning that up? I'm sure they have people whose sole job here is to clean up after you at a place like this."

Out of the corner of her eye, Courtney saw Bo's jaw tighten. She was almost impressed when the next words out of his mouth still maintained a neutral tone. "Actually, this is the staff's break area. They are expected to clean up after themselves here, though it appears to me that it wasn't entirely Courtney's fault that her food wound up on the floor."

He lifted a brow at Daniel, and in that one move, it seemed to Courtney that he'd let the other man know that he was playing in the wrong territory.

Daniel didn't take the hint. Instead, he plowed on into more dangerous waters.

"Courtney, you're eating in the *staff* area?" He glanced at the table of women now openly watching the show they were putting on. "Like, with the *sex workers*?"

Courtney's mouth dropped open, but before she could say anything, Bo's voice landed like a hammer.

"I think you've overstayed your welcome, Mr. Clevins. It seems that it's time for you to go." Bo's booming tone brooked no argument. "William?"

Like magic, William appeared from where he'd been watching from the sidelines of the cafeteria. "What can I do for you, Bo?"

"Please escort Mr. Clevins from the building. I would hate for him to lose his way during his short visit."

"What?" Daniel was finally realizing that his fat mouth had gotten him kicked out. "You can't kick me out! I'm here to visit Courtney! You can't keep her locked up here like a prisoner! She wants to see me!"

He jerked his arm back as William tried to gently lead him away.

"Courtney," Bo boomed, "You're not a prisoner here. Do you want to see Mr. Clevins?"

Still kneeling on the floor, Courtney dropped the piece of

pizza onto the plate that had survived its crash to the hard tile. She looked up at Daniel, giving him a once over. Had she really been with *this* guy for so many years? Why hadn't she seen what a slimeball he was?

She shook her head. "Not particularly."

Bo turned back to Daniel. "There you have it."

At the same time, Daniel stared daggers at Courtney and practically spit, "You bitch. I always thought that you were useless. Turns out I didn't realize your real use was as a whore like these other bitches."

"That's quite enough, Mr. Clevins." Bo boomed. As he spoke, two security guards rounded the corner. Bo nodded to them, then turned back to William. "It seems your assistance won't be needed after all, William. Frank, David: Please escort this *gentleman* from my building. And make sure the rest of your team knows that he's not welcome here again. Ever."

The two men approached Daniel, who immediately put his hands up. "Don't you touch me. I'll sue you so quick, your heads will spin." He turned to Courtney before leaving and said, "I'll see you around." Then he was escorted out of the cafeteria to Courtney's immense relief.

It was short-lived though. To her utter embarrassment, tears threatened to spill down her cheeks. Everyone was still staring. She wanted nothing more than to melt into the ground.

"I'm so sorry, Courtney. He said you two were still together…I just didn't think about it." William knelt beside her and began to help her mop up the pizza sauce and grease from the floor.

Courtney choked back her tears and made her voice steady as she said, "It's okay, William. You didn't know." She tried for a smile but knew as soon as she looked up at the assistant that she wasn't fooling anyone. "He's apparently pretty good at deceiving people."

"Let me take care of this, will you? It's the least I can do."

"I'm supposed to clean up after myself here," Courtney sniffed, decidedly *not* looking up at Bo.

"I know, but I think it'll be okay this one time."

Courtney paused, and when she did, Bo's hand entered her field of vision. He was offering to help her up. After a split moment of hesitation, she took his hand and let herself be pulled up to a stand beside him. Some masochistic notion made her glance around the cafeteria. Most people had gone back to eating but were still glancing up to watch what was left of the show.

"William's right," Bo said, following Courtney's gaze around the room. Curious eyes suddenly found other things to look at. Bo turned his attention back to Courtney, still holding her hand. "I think everyone will forgive you for not cleaning up a mess this one time."

His smile helped to lift her spirits a little, but it was his strong hand around hers that gave her a sense of safety.

She nodded, and Bo led her out of the cafeteria and into the elevator. They were both quiet, and he continued to hold her hand as the elevator began its smooth ascension. Courtney wondered if Bo felt that same underlying pulse of interest she did when the elevator doors closed with just the two of them inside.

She was surprised when they didn't stop at her floor.

Instead, the doors opened on a small octagonal foyer that was decorated in muted hues of beige and olive green. There were two doors, one on either side of the small room. Bo gave Courtney a small almost secret smile and led Courtney, still holding her hand, to the left door. He swiped his access card, and the door popped open.

It was Bo's apartment.

Weirdly, it felt like Courtney had entered the TARDIS. Everything seemed bigger than it should be in here. The ceilings were vaulted with skylights to let in the natural light. A huge sectional couch broke up the open floor plan and provided ample seating around a fireplace that Courtney was sure must be electric. There was a big kitchen with an industrial size stove and a huge island with extra seating to break up the living room from the dining area.

The most breathtaking part was that instead of walls, everywhere she looked were windows, giving them an amazing view of the city around them.

"This is...amazing, Bo. This is your apartment?" It was a stupid question, but she felt like she had to say something as he just stood there, clearly waiting for some sort of reaction to the place.

He cleared his throat a little, as if embarrassed at the opulence of his home. "It is. I mean, not that I'm usually here much. To be honest, I usually spend most of my waking hours—as well as some sleeping ones—in the office next door."

She spotted a shelf full of books and was almost sorry to pull her hand from his to go look. It was probably a bad (not to mention nosy) habit to look at what kind of books people read, but she couldn't help it. As an avid reader herself, she felt like the books people chose were like a window into their very souls.

Too bad I didn't bother looking at Daniel's soul. Might've saved me a lot of trouble. The thought rose unbidden, and she had to tamp it back down so as not to get emotional while standing in the middle of Bo's living room.

His books ranged from philosophy to thrillers. There were a few titles in there that she felt perfectly summed up his public persona like *The Art of War* and *How to Win Friends and Influence People.* But then there were a few revealing gems like *Man's Search for Meaning* that suggested there was a lot more to this man than she'd gotten to know yet.

"I'm really sorry he was able to get into the building and bother you like that." Bo watched Courtney as she perused his library. He liked that the books were the first thing that drew her attention. "It won't happen again," he promised.

"It's okay." She glanced back at him. "Really." Then gave him a slightly watery smile. "Besides if we keep talking about it, I might start really crying, and that would just be embarrassing for both of us."

"Why? You're allowed to have emotions, Courtney."

She turned her back on him, afraid if she kept looking into his dark eyes that she'd either be drawn into that vacuum of need she felt pulling on her or that she really would start crying. With a sigh, she said, "Can't we just talk about something else? I'd rather continue pretending that Daniel never happened."

"Okay." Bo said, watching her delicately pull a limited-edition Mark Twain from the shelf. If it had been anybody else, he would have warned them of its value and asked—okay, demanded—that they put it back.

She gave him a quick glance and proffered the book. "This is a limited edition...I'm surprised you have it just out with the other books where anybody can pick it up."

"With the exception of you, people don't usually pick it up." He watched her ears and neck turn red as she carefully slid the book back into its place on the shelf. He cleared his throat again. At the sound, she turned fully around to face him

Why does she make me so nervous? He wondered.

"Maybe we could...talk about tonight?"

"Okay." Courtney stepped away from the bookshelf and pointed at one part of the sectional. "Mind if I...?"

"No, please. Go ahead."

She plopped down on the couch, and he couldn't help but feel like she somehow belonged there. It was a weird feeling. He almost never spent time in this apartment because, despite the natural light and warm tones, it always felt cold to him somehow.

Now, though, he realized it wasn't the room but rather who was in the room that made the difference. And having Courtney in the space gave it a warmer, more homey feel than he'd ever experienced when Kitty had lived in the suite.

He chose a spot a few feet from her, careful not to get too close but not so far away that he couldn't reach out and touch the warm, smooth skin he ached to caress. "I think Olivia filled you in on tonight's event, yes?"

Courtney tilted her head a little in thought, and he wondered if she even realized she was doing it. "She did. It's a charity event, right?"

"Yes, but there might be..." he paused, searching for the right words to describe what he expected from the evening.

"Drama from an ex?" Her smile was the exact right touch of sardonic.

He let out a bark of laughter before schooling himself, though he couldn't quite suppress a grin. "Yes. That's one way to put it."

Courtney shrugged. "I'm apparently no stranger to that. Though I'll admit, I didn't realize he was like *that* until today."

"Sounds about right." Bo's tone was dry and for just a second, he had this lost look about him before it was suddenly gone again. Tamped down under some innate need to be the strong alpha male. "You think you know a person, and then they show you their true nature."

Courtney remembered the story about his ex, Kitty. Compared to that, Daniel seemed like a walk in the park. She tried to bring the conversation back on track before she gave in to a sudden desire to close the distance between her and Bo. She wanted to erase that lost look from his face forever.

Instead, she shifted the topic. "Speaking of knowing a person, what changed your mind about...this." Courtney gestured between them.

Bo's expression turned wry. "I...I really like you, Courtney. I still want something that's exclusive, but..." He paused as he struggled to find the next words. In an uncharacteristic gesture of nervousness, he smoothed a hand over his perfect hair and fell silent.

When Courtney couldn't take it any longer, she finally prompted. "But...?"

He blew out an almost explosive breath and stood to pace the room, putting space between them. "But, my PR team says you're...good for my image." He glanced over at her as he said this to gauge her reaction.

The excitement in the pit of Courtney's stomach suddenly turned sour. So, Bo hadn't asked her to the charity event because *he* wanted her there. He'd asked her because it would make him look good to have her there on his arm. Not even really eye-candy, but more like social media bait.

"Oh." Courtney wasn't sure what to say other than that.

"I'm sorry. I feel like an asshole even asking you—"

"I mean, technically, you *didn't* ask me. Olivia did. Though she didn't tell me the real reason." Courtney was somewhat impressed by her own cool tone. It wasn't cold. Just carefully neutral.

Bo stopped pacing and gave Courtney his full attention. "I *do* want you there, Courtney. By my side."

"But only for outward appearances."

Bo hesitated, so Courtney pushed on.

"You only want to date me if I'm not dating anyone else. But you're okay with letting the public *think* we're dating when we're not." She wasn't so much making a statement as just feeling out what was going on here. It felt weird and almost hypocritical that he was okay with purposely putting out a false narrative to the public.

"I wouldn't be with anyone else while I was with you. I'd expect both of us to be exclusive." Annoyance tinged his voice. "I don't think I'm asking too much here, Courtney."

Courtney took a deep, steadying breath, then stood. "You're not asking too much, Bo. But you're asking for more than I'm willing to give anyone right now. I don't want to be one of those women who can't stand on their own two feet for five minutes without jumping back into a relationship. I'm using my time here to figure out who I am and what I like."

"And you like Raife."

It felt like he'd slapped her in the face.

"I...." She had to take a moment to collect her thoughts. Had Olivia told him? Surely not. But if Olivia hadn't told him then...

"Have you been digging into my personal information in the OCS?"

His stony expression suggested that she'd hit the nail on the head.

"I see. So, if I won't be exclusive to you, then you'll violate my privacy? Do you think that's okay?"

He opened his mouth to say something, then stopped and closed it again.

Courtney shook her head and headed for the door, avoiding the direct path since it would take her too close to Bo. It meant it took her longer to escape his apartment, but it also gave her time to say, "You know, you're no different than Daniel. Possessive and demanding that I serve your needs. With Daniel, at least what he wanted was straightforward: a girlfriend who would also be his maid. With you, it's worse: it's acting as your puppet and lying to the public for you."

She yanked the door open just as he said, "Courtney, wait."

Her eyes flashed with anger as she spun around. "Don't worry, I'll be at your little event tonight. I already said I'd go, and I'm not one to go back on my word." With that, she stomped out the door and slammed it behind her.

CHAPTER 11

Though Courtney wanted nothing more than to hide in her suite for the rest of the day, she had more appointments to get through before the dreaded charity event.

How am I going to stand by Bo's side tonight and pretend I'm not mad at him? She wondered.

She'd have to employ all the acting skills she'd learned while working as an assistant for Michelle. If she could pretend to like her job and that woman when being constantly demeaned at work, then she could handle pretending to enjoy Bo's company for one night.

The thought made Courtney straighten her back as the make-up artist worked on giving her a smokey eye. They were t-minus forty-five minutes until she'd meet Bo downstairs for their date. And they'd be using the front doors this time rather than leaving through the garage.

Super.

"Okay, remember," Olivia said for like the fifth time, "the press are going to shout all kinds of things at you to get a reaction. Don't let them ruffle your feathers and don't engage."

"I know, Olivia." Courtney tried not to sound exasperated, but it was difficult to keep the annoyance from her voice.

"I'm sorry," the assistant said. "I just want to make sure everything goes well."

"Is this what it would be like all the time if I were really dating, Bo?"

Courtney saw the fleeting look that the make-up artist gave to the woman currently styling Courtney's hair. Whatever. She wasn't trying to keep any secrets here. Plus, she was sure staff had to sign the same NDA she had to keep their mouths shut about what they heard or saw at the Temple.

"Ladies, could you give us a few seconds?" Olivia asked the two women. They quickly vacated the bedroom where Courtney was getting ready in front of the vanity.

Uh oh, I've done it now, Courtney thought. She didn't feel very remorseful though. Then again, it wasn't Olivia's fault that Courtney and Bo weren't exactly getting along.

Olivia leveled a look at Courtney which she probably reserved for the people on her shit list. "What is going on with you today? I know you had a run in with Daniel, but that's no reason for this sudden attitude."

Courtney almost fell into the defensive position of copping more attitude, but then deflated.

"Bo asked me about Raife."

Olivia's head rocked back.

Courtney really didn't want to ask, but she had to know.

"You didn't tell him, did you?" She really hoped Olivia hadn't said anything to Bo. If she had, it would ruin any trust she had in Olivia. She knew that Olivia ultimately worked for Bo, but there were some things you just didn't share with your boss, right?

"I would never tell him something like that, Courtney. That's yours to tell."

"So, does that mean he can look at my private messages in the OCS system?"

Olivia's expression turned dark. "He *shouldn't* be able to do that...then again, part of the privacy statement you signed when you accepted to stay here was that the Temple can gather data on you but won't share it with third parties."

"But, technically, Bo isn't really a third party, is he? I mean, he *is* the company. So, does he look at everyone's information? Or does he just invade the privacy of the women he dates?"

Olivia wasn't sure what to say to that. After a moment she went with, "Bo's never dated a guest here before. Maybe that's why. Maybe the temptation to access your information was too much for him." She sighed. "I'm sorry, Courtney. Are you sure you still want to go tonight? I'd understand if you backed out. Hell, I'm pretty sure Bo would understand. Or he should. Especially if he really did look at your encounters with Raife."

"No. I said I'd go, and I will."

Olivia could tell from the set of Courtney's face that her friend didn't want to talk about it anymore, so she called the hair and make-up stylists back into the room. Rather than spend the next forty minutes in awkward silence, Olivia put some music on in the background. It didn't erase Courtney's anger, but it at least lowered the intensity in the room.

She had selected the black and white halter top gown. Though its neckline was modest, the back had an opening that plunged almost all the way down to her butt. It was almost impossible to wear underwear with it, so she opted not to. The open back made her feel sexy. While putting the gown on, she almost messaged Raife to set up an encounter for later that evening.

The thing that stopped her was the idea that Bo might be monitoring her messages. That and she wasn't sure what time she'd be back from the event. She'd just have to get through the night without looking forward to an encounter with Raife. Maybe when she got back, she could set something up with him for tomorrow.

Before she knew it, it was time to go. Olivia rode the elevator down with her.

"I know you're not happy with Bo," Olivia murmured, "but this evening will be as fun as you let it be. You can still be mad at him while having a good time." She watched Courtney's face for some acceptance of her suggestion, and when she saw none, she went on, "And watch out for Kitty. She is one deceitful bitch. No matter what she says, remember: she is not your friend."

For a split second, Courtney thought, *The enemy of my enemy...*but then, was Bo really her enemy? Or had he just overstepped his reach? She wasn't willing to forgive him yet, but she wasn't willing to side with Kitty against him. Not if Kitty had really set Bo up like Olivia had said.

No, she had a job to do tonight and that was to smile for the cameras that would be downstairs waiting for her.

But Olivia had a point. She could still have a little fun tonight, right?

The smile that Courtney turned on Olivia made the other woman question whether this was a good idea. The elevator doors popped open, revealing a pristine check-in area for guests. Courtney had never been in this front entrance area before since she'd always come and gone via the underground garage. The space was all white marble floors with coppery-gold accents. A few chairs tastefully dotted the lobby in clusters here and there. Courtney doubted anyone ever had the need to use them since the Temple probably ran a very tight check-in process that didn't involve guests seeing each other.

Now that she'd seen the opulent check-in area, she kind of wished it had been part of the experience on her first day here.

Bo stood near the front desk, speaking with the male employee behind the counter.

The opening elevator doors caught his attention, and Courtney saw him stand up just a little straighter when he saw her.

"I'll be fine, Olivia. And so will Bo," Courtney said, then she stepped off the elevator and made a beeline for Bo. Without hesitation she asked him, "Ready?"

His expression suggested that he wanted to say something else, but the situation didn't dictate that he should. "Yes. The driver is waiting outside...along with the press."

"Well, let's not keep them waiting." She turned and offered him her hand. "Might as well keep up the charade."

After an awkward moment, he took it, and Courtney forced herself to ignore the feeling of how *right* her hand felt in his. Not to mention how delicious he looked in his almost form-fitting tux or the way just laying eyes on him had sent a shiver of need down her spine.

Firmly taking her desire for Bo in hand, Courtney moved toward the glazed glass doors and Bo fell into step. Mutely, they marched outside and into a cacophony of reporters and journalists.

Though the sun was only just beginning to set, the photographers were using bright flashes to capture the best pictures possible of the couple as they emerged from the Temple. The brief flashes caught Courtney by surprise for just a moment before she forced herself not to look at them.

The shouting started up as soon as they opened the doors.

"Courtney! Courtney! Over here! Are you and Bo an official item now?"

"Courtney! How long have you and Bo been dating?"

"Bo, what do you think about Kitty Summers being engaged to Ace Lockhart?"

That one was new to Courtney. Though she kept a smile on her face, a quick glance told her that the last question had hit home if she was judging by the slight grimace on Bo's face. She almost felt bad for him.

Almost.

But then she remembered his invasion of her privacy, and she forced herself to keep moving.

They were almost to the waiting SUV when someone nearby shouted, "Courtney! Is it true that you and Bo started seeing each other when you were still with your last boyfriend?"

She couldn't help but swivel toward the woman who had asked that question. Of course, that was like throwing chum in the water. The reporters, or really, paparazzi, she reminded herself because she was pretty sure none of these folks worked for anything more prestigious than the tabloids, started peppering her with questions related to Daniel.

"Is it true you kicked him out of the Temple when Daniel came to confess his love to you?"

"Courtney! Did you sleep with Bo while you were still with Daniel Clevins?"

"Your ex, Daniel Clevins, says you left him penniless and brokenhearted when you left him for Bo and that you were seeing Bo Ryans long before you won the contest! What's your response to this?"

The last was asked by a man who shoved a microphone into Courtney's face. Her automatic response was to jerk back, but not before she opened her mouth to answer.

Sensing an impending statement, a weird hush fell over the reporters closest to the couple.

The sudden quiet somehow made Courtney feel obligated to respond even though Olivia had drummed it into her not to say anything. But the moment she opened her mouth, she knew exactly what she wanted to say.

Looking the reporter dead in the eye, she ignored the camera phone he had on her. "Daniel broke up with me the day I won the contest. I only met Bo after winning. It's true that Bo and I had dinner in New York, as I'm sure you know from the many pictures plastered all over your tabloids, but it was a congratulatory dinner that was strictly business. Only after coming here did Bo and I start dating." She glanced over and up at Bo with what she hoped was the smile of someone newly in love.

Bo correctly responded by returning a sappy grin of his own.

"That's all I have to say on the matter," Courtney finished. They closed the distance to the car then they were speeding off to the casino.

"It's not a great idea to talk to them," Bo commented without emotion. "No matter what you say, they'll just twist your words and somehow you'll wind up the bad guy."

"I'll keep that in mind." Courtney kept her gaze out the window. She didn't like that things were this awkward between them but wasn't willing to pretend things were fine. Sure, she'd do that for the cameras and for the public at the event tonight, but there was no reason to pretend anything while they were alone.

"Are you going to be like this the whole night?"

She whipped her head around. "You mean, am I going to continue being angry at you for invading my privacy? Yes. Yes I am." She tried to settle back against the leather seats but was too livid to relax. "I'll play the game for the cameras, but

I don't have to pretend to be happy with you when it's just the two of us."

"You didn't have to come tonight."

"I said I would, and I don't go back on my promises."

There was another few moments of awkward silence before they thankfully pulled up to the casino.

"Courtney," Bo said, touching her arm before she could open the door to get out. His touch made her hesitate. She looked back and lifted a brow in question.

He sighed. "I...I should have said this earlier, but I didn't invade your privacy."

"Oh really?" Could her eyebrows possibly get any higher on her forehead? "Then how did you know about Raife?"

Bo opened his mouth to answer but before he could, the door was yanked open by an attendant and Courtney was helped out of the vehicle. His chance to erase Courtney's anger with him had just disappeared, and now he knew he'd be in for a long night of pretend happiness from Courtney and real ass-kissing from the other attendees. The two things he hated the most. Great.

* * *

EVERYONE INSIDE WAS DRESSED to the nines. The women wore a variety of black and white dresses and made up for the lack of color with bright jewelry that winked in the low lighting. The men wore expensive black tuxes and bow ties with little difference between them. Apparently big money seemed to require giving up all individuality.

Courtney looked down at her own black and white gown, half-glad that Olivia had helped her dress appropriately but also slightly tempted to go change into something more colorful to galvanize what she assumed would be a snooty crowd.

Then again, she already felt like she was living in a fairy tale lately. No reason to stand out like the proverbial princess.

It's not like she had come with Prince Charming, after all.

Casino staff, mostly women, Courtney noted, milled around serving flutes of champagne and hor d'oeuvres. Courtney snatched a flute off the first passing tray and took a gulp. If she was going to have to be here, then she would at least try and have a good time.

Seeing Courtney's champagne, Bo spied a bar set up at the side of the crowded room. "I'm going to get a drink. Do you want something stronger than that?" He pointed at Courtney's drink.

"I'm fine with this, thanks."

He nodded then turned and melted into the crowd, leaving Courtney on her own among a sea of rich strangers. She smiled at those who made eye contact with her but was too unsure of herself to approach any of the groups.

It was going to be a long night if she just stood around sipping champagne by herself the whole time.

A cheer from the corner caught her attention. A group of people had gathered around, blocking her view of what was over there. Rather than continuing to stand there looking ridiculous, she decided to go see what everyone was so interested in.

She approached the group and stood next to an older black woman wearing a wine-red form fitting dress that Courtney could only tell was red when she stepped closer. The woman had a real air of nobility Courtney hadn't gotten from the other guests. The woman offered Courtney a welcoming smile.

Courtney smiled nervously back. "What's going on over here?"

"Roulette. Wanna give it a go?" She jerked her head, and

suddenly Courtney could see the table as a couple strolled away.

"I'm happy watching, but thanks," she told the other woman.

"Oh, come on. It's easy. And I bet with a young woman like you beside me, I'll have better luck." She stepped up to the table. "What do you think, go big and put it all on one number?"

Her sudden grin was contagious. Courtney couldn't help but smile back and take a step closer. She looked down at the table with its black and red wheel at the other end.

"Hmm, you might want to start small first," Courtney noted since she had no idea what else to say.

The woman winked at her. "Good idea." To a young man beside her, she said, "Let's put two-hundred on red like the young woman says."

As the man pulled chips from a tray he held, Courtney said, "Two-hundred dollars seems a bit much, don't you think?"

The woman turned back to her. "Two hundred dollars? Oh no, dear. That's two-hundred *thousand* dollars. But don't worry. Anything we win goes toward the charity, and if we lose, well, the casino has promised to donate that as well."

Courtney caught her breath. She knew the people here had money or they wouldn't be here, but two-hundred thousand dollars seemed a ridiculous amount of money to just gamble away! She could buy a house with that much!

She also realized she'd have no way to play any of the games here. Not with those kinds of stakes.

The woman was still watching Courtney as she took the chips from the young man and placed them on the table, so Courtney smiled and said, "Oh. Um...good luck?"

The dealer started the ball and wheel spinning. Courtney held her breath, sure she'd just jinxed the woman.

Finally, after what felt like forever, the ball fell on a red eight.

The woman jerked her head at Courtney and elbowed the young man. "See? What'd I tell you? She's a good luck charm. How about another round? And why not be a little riskier this time? How about a split bet between two numbers?"

Courtney fumbled for how to politely back out of the situation and, seeing this, the woman shook her head. "We've already donated the money to charity, so it's not like we'd really be losing anything. Anything we win also just gets donated. It's a win-win for everybody."

"Alright," Courtney said in semi-mocking resignation. She took another step forward to get a better look at the table. "How about… eight and nine…?"

"Eight and nine it is. Same amount?" The woman asked with a glitter of excitement in her eyes. When Courtney nodded, she signaled to the young man who placed the chips on the line between the two numbers.

The wheel spun.

Courtney clutched her champagne glass, not daring to breathe.

"Eight!" The dealer—or croupier, as Courtney remembered from her gambling lessons—called out.

The woman gave Courtney an appraising look. "See? I knew you were good luck the moment I laid eyes on you. I'm Hattie by the way," she stuck out her perfectly manicured hand, "Hattie Singleton."

"Courtney," she responded, taking the woman's strong hand in her own.

"It's a pleasure to meet you, Courtney." Hattie let her hand go. "What's our next bet, young lady?"

Caught up in the game, Courtney stepped up beside her, forgetting her nervousness. They lost money on the next round when she bet on another single number, but she made up for it by betting more safely on all odd numbers and gained some of their winnings back.

She was on a winning streak when a hand dropped on her shoulder, surprising her.

"There you are," Bo's deep voice snuck under her defenses and gave her a warm, fuzzy feeling before she remembered that she was still pissed at him.

"This nice woman is helping me learn roulette." Courtney turned to indicate Hattie beside her.

Hattie let out a deep belly laugh. "This young lady is helping this old woman win a lot of money. It's only too bad we don't get to keep it."

"I leave you alone for five minutes, and you manage to find the only other self-made billionaire in the room?" Bo shook his head, but the grin on his lips grew larger as he took Hattie's hand in his and bent to brush a kiss over the back of it.

"I haven't seen you in a while, Ryans. What have you been up to?" Hattie asked when she'd reclaimed her hand.

"Oh, you know. A little of this, a little of that."

Hattie leaned in. "I heard a rumor you were doing more in New York than picking up this young lady."

"Oh?" Bo raised his eyebrows, all innocence. "I'm not sure what you mean."

"I'm sure you don't. But if you *are* up to what I *think* you're up to, let an old woman know. New York has a lot more to offer than Vegas does these days. There's only so many roulette, craps, and poker rounds a woman can play before it all kind of loses its meaning. I'd take a Broadway show and dinner at Momofuku any day of the week over another game of blackjack." She turned her attention to Courtney. "But you made this game a lot more interesting, young lady. I thank you for that. Hopefully dinner will happen soon, and then I can go home and sit with my dog and have a proper whiskey without all these prying eyes and ears." She waved a hand around.

Courtney looked up and caught several other guests watching their threesome before eyes hastily looked away. She hadn't realized they'd been being watched. Or maybe they'd only started staring when Bo walked up.

"Bets?" The croupier said with a slightly annoyed tone to let them know that they were holding up his game.

"I think we're done," Courtney said quickly.

At the same time, Hattie said, "Oh, how about just one more round before I lose all your luck to this big galoot." She hooked a thumb at Bo.

Bo's mouth turned down at the slight which, of course, made Courtney smile as Hattie had intended.

"Sure. Why not?" Courtney shrugged and turned her attention back to the roulette table. "We can bet on zero, right?"

"We can…" Hattie's neutral tone suggested that it wasn't a great idea, but it wasn't like she got to take the money home, so Courtney figured what the hell.

"Okay, how about fifty on zero?"

"As you wish, my lady." Hattie winked at her and took the chip from her assistant, placing it on the square with the zero in it. When she turned back to Courtney, she said, "Nothing like taking a lotta risk with a little money, right?"

The croupier gave the no more bets signal and started the wheel and ball spinning. Courtney glanced over at the game nervously. "I guess if a charity gets it all anyways, it doesn't matter, right?"

"Right you are," Hattie murmured, just as mesmerized by the game as Courtney was.

The ball fell into the wheel and began its manic staccato dance. The wheel's rotation finally started to slow. Courtney's mouth dropped open as the ball dropped into the zero slot on the wheel.

"Well, well, well." Hattie stared at Courtney, eyes narrowed in inspection. "You truly are a lucky one to have around." She turned to Bo whose wide eyes were also flicking between the board and Courtney. "Didn't know what you had there, didja, Ryans? You're lucky I didn't turn on my charm and steal her away from you. It would serve you right for leaving her alone in a room full of sharks."

Bo hid his surprise behind one of his ever-ready business masks. "I suppose you're right, Hattie. What table have they got you at for dinner tonight?"

"I'm not sure" She turned to the young man with her who was hastily retrieving their winnings. "Matt?"

The man turned. "Oh, um, table seven I believe."

"Pity. We're at table four," Bo said with real regret. "It would have been nice to sit with you and your grandson." Here he dipped his head at Matt in greeting, "and have a conversation we'd actually enjoy."

"Surely you're not saying you don't enjoy the lady's company?" Hattie inclined her head toward Courtney.

Bo backpedaled. "Of course not. It's just—"

"I'm only teasing, Ryans! Relax."

"Wait," Courtney said, looking between the two. "You donate a ton of money, and then you don't get to pick where you sit?"

"No," the two grunted in unison.

To Courtney, Hattie said, "It was lovely meeting you, young lady. Keep this one on his toes, wouldja?" She jerked her head at Bo and gave Courtney a wicked grin. Her expression suddenly shifted to distaste as she saw someone over Bo's shoulder. "Looks like a good time to find somewhere else to be." She gave Bo a mock bow. "Good night and good luck, Ryans." As she walked away, her grandson trailing behind her, Courtney heard her mutter, "You're gonna need it."

Courtney scanned the room for what had prompted the last remark and Hattie's sudden shift in demeanor. A woman who stood out from the crowd made a beeline toward Bo. She wore a vivacious red dress that left little to the imagination. In fact, it looked more like something that Courtney would wear to a private encounter at the Temple than out in public, but everybody had a different comfort level, she supposed. Unlike Hattie's tasteful wine-red dress that blended in with the crowd, this woman was clearly working hard to stand out. The woman's bright blond hair had been expertly styled in a complicated braid that lent some sophistication to her ensemble.

Courtney's immediate impression was that the woman was trying to be the sexiest and most interesting person in the room. Unfortunately, though she did stand out, it was for all the wrong reasons if the disapproving looks following in her wake were any indication.

The woman practically dragged a man along behind her. Though he was better dressed for the occasion than the woman, his demeanor also screamed "trying-too-hard."

"Heads up," Courtney murmured with barely any movement of her lips. She pasted on a fake smile as the woman reached Bo and tapped him on the shoulder to get his attention.

Bo's eyes met Courtney's, and she caught the dark look that barely concealed desperation before he turned with his own fake smile.

"Kitty. What a surprise." Bo's dry tone sounded more like someone who'd just noticed a guest tracking mud through their house.

"Bo!" Kitty exclaimed a little loudly while leaning in for a hug that Bo haltingly returned. "It's so nice to see you!" The hug lasted a little longer than Courtney would have been comfortable with if Kitty were hugging her. If Courtney and Bo were really dating, she would have felt that Kitty's hug lingered a little too long for someone who was just supposed to be an ex-girlfriend.

But we aren't *dating,* she sternly reminded herself.

Finally, when Kitty pulled back from Bo, she glanced over at Courtney. Was it just Courtney's imagination, or was there anger and jealousy in those bright blue eyes?

"Who's your date, Bo?"

Courtney decided to save Bo the trouble. "I'm Courtney." She stuck out her hand, forcing the other woman to shake or appear awkward. After the look Kitty had given her, Courtney much preferred a handshake than risk the possibility of Kitty stabbing her in the back while giving her a hug.

"So nice to meet you," Kitty gushed. It was a little over the top.

Had Bo really fallen for this lady's fake act? Courtney wondered. But Olivia had apparently been taken in too which led Courtney to conclude that the woman must have dropped most of the charade now that she was no longer with Bo.

Suddenly, Kitty stepped back and, with a big, go-fuck-yourself grin, put her arm around the man she'd dragged over.

"Bo, you remember Ace Lockhart, don't you?"

Courtney did a double take. *This* was Ace Lockhart? The preening man looked more like he'd try to sell you a pyramid scheme or a timeshare than a multi-millionaire who owned Carnal Temptations.

Bo stepped forward and shook hands with Ace. "Nice to see you again."

"What's it been, two years since we were last in the same

room?" Ace's smirk should have warned Courtney of his next words. "It was in court, right? For the lawsuit you lost to me?"

Courtney barely managed to keep from sucking in a surprised breath. She noticed that Ace had waited until Bo dropped his hand before adding that last part. Maybe he was afraid that Bo might physically retaliate by crushing his hand? Courtney wouldn't blame Bo if he did.

Before Bo could respond, Kitty gave a tittering laugh like a 1950's housewife. "Oh, Ace. Don't be crass." Then, like a shark homing in on blood in the water, she fixed Courtney with a smile that seemed a little maniacal.

"How did you two meet?"

Since she was clearly asking her and not Bo, Courtney smiled and stepped closer to Bo. He took the hint and put his free arm around her back. "I won the contest to stay at Pleasure Temple. When I got there, I just kept bumping into this big guy." She smiled up at Bo and was a little surprised at the little jolt of attraction that hit her when he gazed down at her.

She had to force her attention back to Kitty whose jaw looked like it might snap from clenching so hard.

"He finally asked me out to a real dinner date and the rest is history."

As if on cue, Bo squeezed her to him, then leaned down and brushed a brief kiss over her lips.

Her brain short-circuited for a moment and all she wanted to do was find a private space where she could let go, forget her anger, and kiss him back.

But she was still mad, damn it.

Remembering they had an audience, she turned back, a little red-cheeked now, to Kitty and Ace.

"Isn't that sweet." Kitty said, but if looks could kill, Courtney would have melted into the floor like the wicked witch. To Bo, Kitty said, "I'm so glad you settled for someone, Bo, rather than being alone forever after our difficult breakup."

It was all Courtney could do to keep from telling the woman to piss off.

"And just think," Kitty continued, "we're at the same table tonight, so we'll get to catch up over dinner." She held Bo's eyes for another second before turning back to Courtney. "I can tell you *all* the gossip on this one." Then her voice dropped, and her lips twisted into a sexually charged smile. "I know *all* his secrets."

"How...interesting." Courtney finally said when she could think of no other description to use. "Well, it was nice to meet you. It sounds like we'll see you in a bit. Bo said he'd play me at a little blackjack, so we're off to fulfill his promise."

With that, she carted Bo off before the other couple could protest.

CHAPTER 12

*W*hen they were safely tucked into a quiet corner and out of earshot from the rest of the guests, Courtney finally spoke her mind. "We are *not* eating with them. She is clearly an awful person." She looked up at Bo, who looked faintly embarrassed at Kitty's behavior, so she added, "Not that I can say much about dating awful people. Not after you met Daniel earlier."

Bo's expression smoothed out. "He *was* kind of an asshole. To be honest, I was kind of surprised that you were with him." He paused for a moment, deciding whether or not to continue, then said, "What did you see in him, anyways?"

Courtney sighed. *What* had *she seen in him?* She wondered to herself. "I dunno. He was great when we first started dating. Flowers, texts, attention...and then it was like he just didn't try anymore. I'm not sure when he went from being just uninterested in me to being a total dick." Courtney shrugged. "What about you? What made you start dating Kitty?"

Now it was Bo's turn to sigh. He took a quick swig of his quickly disappearing whiskey before saying. "About the same. She seemed interesting and was fun. She asked me questions about my interests and listened to what I said. It took me a while to realize that she didn't really have any interests of her own. If I took an interest in something, she immediately did, too. It would have been fine except she started to feel a little fake. Eventually it felt like she was just there with me all the time to make sure I didn't take an interest in other women. When I started to make time just for myself, that made her cling to me even harder. Then the marriage talk started." He shuddered. "I'm not against marriage, but...it just didn't feel *right* with her."

Courtney downed the rest of her champagne. "I get it. I always thought it was inevitable that I would marry Daniel one day, but I never pushed him to ask because...I guess I just wasn't really that excited about the prospect of marrying him. Huh." It was odd to realize that here and now. "I guess we both dodged a bullet, huh?"

A staff member appeared before Courtney like magic, taking her empty glass and handing her a fresh flute of champagne. When he was gone, Courtney held her glass out to Bo.

"Here's to breaking it off with shitty partners."

He clinked his glass against hers. "Here, here."

They were quiet for a moment, sipping their drinks before Courtney stated, "Just so you know, I'm still mad at you. But other than Hattie, you're the only person here that I know, so we'll just have to get through this night together." She looked out at the crowd, watching as Kitty loudly spoke to another couple who looked like they wanted to be anywhere else but there.

"One thing's for sure, we are not going to sit with Kitty and Ace tonight," she added as she scanned the room. "Who did you get our table number from?"

Bo's brows drew down for a brief second, then he leaned

in close to Courtney and, using the hand holding the whiskey glass, he pointed across the room. "See the woman over there by the double doors?"

He was so close that his breath moved a tendril of hair, tickling Courtney's neck. It, along with his close proximity made her want to pull him close again. Instead, she forced herself to nod, and he stepped away, putting space between them again. She sternly reminded herself that she was still angry at him and kept her hands to herself.

"She's got the list of seat assignments," Bo said. He'd caught a whiff of Courtney's subtle perfume mixed with the vanilla scent of her shampoo. It had been a bit of a struggle to step away, but he'd forced himself to do it. He might not be guilty of what Courtney thought he was, but that didn't mean her anger was misplaced. Just that she was mad at him for the wrong thing.

"Got it." Courtney gave him a quick appraising and saw some emotion flicker through his expression before she could identify it. If they'd been a real couple, she would have asked about it. Instead, she asked, "Will you be okay while I go work my personal assistant magic and get us a different table?"

"I'll be fine, but thanks for the concern."

Courtney couldn't tell if he was annoyed or amused, so she just nodded and left him to fend for himself.

The thing about being a personal assistant was that sometimes you had to take care of difficult tasks that required a little bit of persuasion. Courtney had once had to sweet talk her boss's way onto a booked flight. That little bit of magic had actually involved booting another first-class passenger, yet Courtney had accomplished it.

It also occasionally involved telling a few white lies.

As she approached the woman Bo had pointed out, she

recognized some clear signs of severe stress as the woman stared down at her clipboard with wide, panicked eyes. Uh oh. In Courtney's experience with event planning, this was how she would personally react to being asked to move someone to a different table.

It looked like someone had already been making requests to switch tables. Hmm.

Courtney shifted her initial plan of addressing the situation head on and decided instead to try a simpler route.

Making her voice as warm as possible, Courtney said, "Hi. I couldn't help but notice you seem a bit stressed out. Is everything okay?"

Before looking up, the woman said, "Why does everyone always wait until the last minute to demand changes to the seating arrangement? Dinner starts in ten minutes!" With that, she looked up and a look of shocked horror crossed her face as she recognized Courtney and realized she'd just spoken her inner thoughts out loud.

"I mean," she quickly backtracked and schooled her features into a mask of calm, "is there something I can help you with?"

"Actually, I was going to ask you the same thing." Before the woman could brush Courtney off, she quickly added, "As a personal assistant who's organized many an event, you seem like someone who's been thrown one of those last minute, curveball demands. Maybe I can help by switching seats with someone?"

The woman opened her mouth to tell Courtney that she had a handle on it but changed her mind at the last second. "Actually...you're Courtney Bliss, right?"

"Yup. That's me." Courtney smiled.

The woman glanced down at her clipboard, then back up at Courtney. "Weird, I just got a request for someone who wants to sit at your table, but there aren't any seats left. I was told to arrange things by the highest donation and, of course, as I'm sure you know, Bo Ryans made the biggest donation tonight. He's supposed to be at the front table."

Courtney hadn't known that, but it also didn't surprise her. Bo didn't seem to mind giving away his money as long as it was for a good cause. She liked that about him…

Still mad, she reminded herself.

"But…" Courtney prompted.

"But we just got a big donation from a couple, and they asked to be moved to that table."

Realization suddenly hit Courtney. "Let me guess, Ace Lockhart just made a big donation and asked to be moved to our table."

"How did you know it was him?"

Courtney couldn't help but glance back at the crowd of guests milling around the game floor. She wasn't surprised when she found Kitty Summers staring daggers in her direction. Of course, as soon as Kitty had figured out what table she and Bo were assigned to, she'd gotten Ace to make a big donation so she could sit at their table and ruin Bo and Courtney's night.

What a total bitch, Courtney thought, *but two can play at that game.*

With a grin she couldn't keep off her face, she turned back to the woman with the clipboard.

"You know, Bo doesn't mind switching tables. He doesn't really want that kind of recognition for his donation anyways." Courtney had no idea if that was true but pressed on. "We'd be happy to switch places with them if that helps your seating arrangement."

"Really? Are you sure?" The woman seemed to be fighting the need to just take Courtney's offer.

"Of course. It's really no problem. What table should we go to instead?"

The woman let out a huge sigh of relief. "Table eight. Thank you so much for switching. I really appreciate it. Please thank Mr. Ryans as well."

"Of course," Courtney said again. "Happy to help."

With that, she made her way back to Bo who raised an eyebrow at the huge grin of triumph on her face. When she got close enough, he said, "Careful with that smile, or people will think you're up to something."

Courtney laughed. "I am up to something." More conspiratorially, she leaned in and told him, "We'll now be dining at table eight." Her grin grew wider as she couldn't help but add, "We're actually switching places with Kitty and Ace."

Bo let out a short bellow of laughter before he could reign himself in. "They demanded to move to our table when they heard where we were sitting, didn't they?"

Courtney nodded, "And he made a *big* donation to do it."

Looking like a schoolboy who'd just pulled a particularly sneaky prank, Bo hid a grin behind his whiskey glass. "How very kind of him."

Their evening went much better after that, and Courtney had to continually remind herself that she was still angry at Bo. He just had that charm that made it difficult to stay mad at him. She found it maddeningly frustrating.

At dinner, he guided her to their table with a gentle hand on the small of her back and pulled out a chair for her. The smoldering look he gave her when she sat made her want to touch him, and she couldn't help but brush her fingers lightly against his when he sat before pulling back into her own space again.

The other guests at their table seemed delighted that Bo and Courtney would be joining them and that, paired with the fact that they now sat at the table beside Hattie's, made for a more enjoyable night. The older woman continually turned and regaled them and her own table with stories of all the mistakes she'd made when starting up her distillery business.

At one point, while laughing at one of Hattie's stories, she found herself putting a hand on Bo's arm. His response was a questioning look, and when she didn't immediately pull away, he took her hand and held it in his until the end of the story.

Dinner wrapped up with a decadent dessert, and then the guests were released for another two hours of gambling if they wished.

"How about that game of blackjack you mentioned earlier?" Bo asked with true hope in his voice.

"Okay. I might actually beat you after all the lessons I've had."

His mouth twisted in mock disbelief. "We'll see." Then he smiled again to show he was joking.

Courtney was at war with herself over liking Bo. She felt like she should still be giving him the cold shoulder for invading her privacy like that, but she couldn't very well do that while trying to convince a room full of people that they were a real couple in love.

The other problem was that she simply didn't *want* to be mad at Bo anymore.

As they sat at the blackjack table, she caught Bo giving her a look out of the corner of his eye, then his head snapped over completely to look at someone behind her.

Courtney's stomach clenched, knowing exactly who could elicit that kind of response from Bo. She forced a polite smile as she turned.

Kitty smoothly sat in the chair beside her at the blackjack table. Ace was nowhere to be seen.

"We missed you at dinner. I guess you decided to skimp a little on the donations this year, huh, Bo?" She leaned across Courtney as if she weren't there. "You can tell me the truth, you know. Has it been a difficult few years for you now that you have to compete against Ace's company?"

As Courtney watched, a muscle began to twitch in Bo's cheek. For someone who could handle multimillion dollar business transactions, she was a little surprised by how easily he let Kitty get to him.

Then again, matters of the heart were always a little more difficult than business.

"Actually," Courtney said, leaning forward while pretending to adjust the strap on her shoes and using the movement to force Kitty back into her own space, "we decided to give someone else our seats." She dropped her voice to a whisper, "I guess someone dropped a large donation so they could sit at the front table and make a display of how much money they'd donated. Some people, huh?" She turned her attention back to Bo so she didn't have to see the other woman's reaction. "How do we get chips, Bo? I'd like to play."

Bo waved one of the staff over, and after a quick discussion, the man left then quickly returned with two trays of chips. Bo thanked him and handed one tray to Courtney.

"Still feeling lucky from the roulette tables?"

"I am, actually." Courtney couldn't seem to keep the smile off her face when she looked at Bo. And it wasn't even for the sake of pissing off Kitty, though that was an added benefit. No, she just liked the way he looked at her. The way he listened attentively, how his eyes glittered, and how the corners of his mouth turned up when she made him laugh.

Kitty's tinkly voice cut across her thoughts, "Are we going to play, or are you two going to flirt all night?"

"We're ready," Courtney said to the dealer, completely ignoring Kitty.

The first two rounds, Courtney played it safe and ended up squandering her chips away when Kitty got closer than any of them to twenty-one but didn't bust. The third round, Bo won. After that, Courtney decided to be a little more daring, but she overshot and ended up busting.

Though she was losing Bo's money, it was hard to care very much when she knew all of it was going toward charity. Even with Kitty sitting beside her, Courtney was still enjoying herself—mostly because Bo was there keeping the game fun and interesting.

"Are you sure you want to do that?" He asked her at one point. She'd asked for another card though she already had a Jack on the table, putting her close to the threshold for busting.

"I'm trying to live on the edge here," Courtney said back, flushing a little as she caught his eyes on her lips. She unconsciously licked them and watched as he took in a short breath in reaction. She gave him a wicked grin. "Plus, it's your money, so I'm not out anything. If anything, I'm like a modern-day Robin Hood. Taking from the sinful rich and giving to charity."

"Hmm. This might be a dangerous way to start your gambling experience if it doesn't have any real stakes for you."

Courtney started to respond then hesitated. Did she really want to up the ante and risk a repeat of their moment in the elevator? The hot and heavy part, hell yes. But the part where she got shut down by him when she refused to be exclusive? Not so much.

Still, he'd been so attentive all night. He was clearly still interested in her. Throughout the evening, her sharp anger at having her privacy violated by him had been worn down to a dull edge. Now she just wanted an explanation. Or a promise that it wouldn't happen again.

When it was obvious that she'd hesitated for too long, she finally blurted out, "Let's make this more interesting, then. How about whichever of us comes closest to 21 without going over in this next hand gets to..." she paused for a moment remembering that they had an audience and were supposed to be happily dating. "Whoever wins gets to decide what we do for the rest of the night."

Though it might sound lame to their audience, Courtney had a feeling Bo would understand what she was asking. If she won, she would tell Bo that she wanted to stay with him for the night, no strings attached. She wasn't sure what he would ask for if he won, but by the terms she'd set, he wouldn't be able to demand exclusivity if they were only together for one night.

As she watched him considering the bet, she got the distinct feeling that he understood exactly how she'd backed him into a corner. He only confirmed it by saying, "Aren't you the negotiator?" His hand went to his chin for a moment in that way that made Courtney want to place her hand over his and lean in for a kiss.

"Bets?" The dealer said, clearly waiting. Even Kitty hadn't placed her bet yet, too busy listening to the exchange between Bo and Courtney.

"I'll accept that wager," Bo finally agreed, sending a little thrill through Courtney.

Suddenly the game was a lot more interesting. They placed actual bets on the table again and waited for their cards.

Bo got a King and a seven while Courtney was dealt an eight and a ten.

The dealer ended up with a queen, but it didn't matter to them. Though they had money on the table, they weren't trying to beat the dealer. They were really only playing between themselves this time.

In this game, Courtney would have the advantage since Bo would get his card first and she would know what it was before she had to decide whether to stay or ask for another card.

They measured each other up somewhat mockingly for their audience while in actuality they were truly trying to determine how the other person would play. Courtney had moved to the edge of her seat and was biting her lip slightly while Bo tapped a single finger on his leg. They noticed each other's nervous ticks and both broke into a smile.

A roguish look passed over Bo's face, and Courtney realized she knew exactly what he was going to say before he opened his mouth.

"Hit me," Bo told the dealer then flicked his eyes back to Courtney.

He was trying to lose. He knew what she would ask for, and he was trying to lose.

He wanted to spend the night with her just as much as she did. By letting her win, it gave him permission to let go of his expectation for an exclusive relationship for just this one night.

Her heart beat faster. If she could win this, she could have Bo Ryans all to herself for the night. Somehow, it was a little more thrilling than the idea of an exclusive relationship with him. Though, to be honest, that had a certain allure as well... until she remembered her passionate encounters with Raife.

At least with their bet, she wouldn't have to make the decision to give that up just yet regardless of who won.

The dealer placed Bo's third card on the table. A Queen of hearts.

He'd busted.

Courtney put a hand over her cards and told the dealer, "I'll stay."

Neither of them watched the rest of the game or how Kitty won the hand. To them, the only person who had won was Courtney.

"Well," Bo said, his deep voice feeling almost like a caress, "What do you have in mind for the rest of our evening?"

"I think I'm done with cards for the night. You?"

"I'm at your command, my lady." He took her hand and brushed a light kiss over it, sending jolts of electricity through her and making her mouth suddenly very dry.

A loud, overdramatic groan came from the other side of Courtney.

When Courtney turned to Kitty, the woman said, "Get a room, will you?" She was clearly trying to make Courtney feel embarrassed.

Instead, Courtney broke into a smile, knowing it would annoy Kitty. "I think we'll do just that." Swiveling back to Bo, who still had a hold of her hand, she said, "Are you ready to go, or do we need to stay awhile longer?"

"I'm ready."

The clear desire in his eyes suggested he was ready for a lot more than just leaving.

Courtney turned her hand in his so she could squeeze it as she stood. To Kitty, she said, "Great game, Kitty. It was so nice to meet you and Ace."

Kitty put on a fake smile causing Courtney to wonder again how Bo hadn't managed to see right through the woman.

"And you as well," Kitty said though her tone suggested otherwise.

Not my problem, Courtney thought and turned her back on the woman to look up at Bo.

"Let's get out of here," he said. At her nod, they left the table, deposited their chips with a staff member, and left.

Maybe it was the champagne, but the whole time, Courtney felt like she was walking on air. She wasn't sure she'd ever been quite so excited to put her hands on a man before. And that included her encounters with Raife.

Tonight was going to be something. That was for sure.

CHAPTER 13

On the ride back to the Temple, they made out like teenagers. Hot and heavy yet also giggly. Or at least, Courtney was giggly. She was pretty sure Bo would have been completely okay with having sex in the back of the car, but she certainly wasn't. Not with the driver right there. Even making out with Bo in the back of the SUV was a little embarrassing since she knew they had an audience.

As usual, the driver dropped them off in the parking garage near the elevator. They separated long enough for Courtney to smooth down her dress and Bo to unmuss his hair, making themselves presentable for the thirty second walk to the elevator door while holding hands. The staff member manning the elevator greeted them and hit the call button while Bo made awkward conversation.

Or maybe it was only awkward to her because she desperately wanted Bo's soft yet demanding lips back on hers again.

After what felt like an eternity, the elevator came. When the doors snicked shut and the car started its trek to the top floor, they were finally alone. Bo squeezed Courtney's hand

and slowly drew her to him, giving her time to pull away if she wanted.

What she wanted was Bo.

But…

She looked up and nearly drowned in those dark eyes of his. Biting her lip for a second, she put a hand to his chest and paused his motion of leaning in to kiss her. Doubt drew a curtain over his eyes and, not liking the way that made her feel, Courtney quickly asked, "Are you sure you want to do this?"

"A bet's a bet." His hand, warm against her exposed back, moved up and down slightly as he spoke. She wanted so much to give in. To push him against the elevator wall and have her way with him.

But…

"I know I won the bet, but are you sure you're okay with this?" She freed her hand from his hip for just a moment to gesture at them. "I'm not agreeing to more than just tonight." She smiled, a little embarrassed but also proud that she was willing to be so open with her desires. "I really, *really* want this tonight. But if you're not sure you can handle that—"

He pulled her against him, making her gasp into his mouth as he kissed her fiercely. His sudden need sent a thrill through her. His hands roved her body, moving from her back, down to squeeze her butt while simultaneously pulling her against him.

She could feel how hard he was. Her body responded, wanting him to take her like Raife would.

But this is Bo, she reminded herself. She needed to be ready for a different kind of sex. Her mind flashed on what she remembered from the sex tape of him and Kitty. The idea of being in Kitty's position thrilled her, but she wasn't sure how to ask for that from him.

The doors opened to Bo's foyer, and he automatically

began walking them toward his apartment. It was awkward as hell, but Courtney didn't care. She didn't want his hands to leave her body or his lips to leave hers.

He fumbled for the keycard in his wallet and finally swiped it against the scanner after what felt like a million years. When they'd crossed the threshold, he kicked the door shut behind them. She suddenly wished she'd worn a different dress. Sure, it had a plunging back, but it was really too long and tight around the hips and legs for this kind of thing.

Damn it! She pulled back from Bo, taking in a big gasp of air and turned her back to him.

"Unzip me?"

Rather than quickly complying as she expected, he pulled her butt against him and cupped her breasts, dropping kisses on her exposed neck, then down her back, following the opening of the dress. He had to shift to continue down, pulling his hardness away from her. She missed the pressure, but his ever-moving lips and tongue more than made up for it.

Oh, my, yes! Was her thought as he straightened back up and leaned her over the back of the couch. He unzipped her dress, making it a little looser, then snaked his hand through the opening and around her front. She'd forgotten she hadn't worn underwear with the dress and moaned when he rubbed his finger oh-so-gently against her clitoris.

"Like this?" He breathed quietly in her ear.

"Yes," she gasped as he pressed against her from behind, the fabric of her dress and his pants annoyingly still between them. She rocked her hips back and upwards toward him. He responded by moved his finger against that sweet spot, sending a pulse of need through her.

"I want you inside me," she demanded, breathing hard.

With one hand still pleasuring her from the front, he used

his other hand to unzip his pants and hike up her dress. He pushed her a little farther forward on the couch, putting her on her tiptoes, then guided himself inside her from behind while still rubbing her clitoris.

She cried out but pushed herself up against him, driving him further inside. He leaned forward, his other hand now free again to delve down the top of her dress at an awkward angle to gently squeeze her breast. He slowed things down. Pulling out and pausing his finger from rubbing that sweet spot before slowly filling her up again and moving his finger to send that jolt of need through her. She gasped and bucked her hips back against him.

He slowed their pace still further, and she wondered if she would just explode with need. She could hear him gasping in pleasure as well each time he slid back inside her, and she wondered how she could get him to speed up. But he was entirely in charge of this experience, and that was what made it delicious in her opinion.

"Is this what you want?" His gravelly voice said in her ear as he paused partially inside her.

"Yes," she said, and he slid all the way in causing her words to turn into a moan.

Courtney tried to focus on the push and pull, gasping in pleasure each time Bo touched her. That now-familiar pressure began to build inside her even at this slow pace. Her breathing began to follow his slow, yet deep thrusts.

Just before she felt herself nearing the crest of that pressure, Bo quickly sped up and switched to staying inside her after each thrust. The hand squeezing her breast slid up to cover her mouth. She panted and moaned into it. The sudden visual she had of him pinning her to the couch while taking her from behind mixed with her encounters with Raife and completely overwhelmed her synapses.

His next thrust and finger movement sent her over the

edge. She cried out at what felt like explosions in her body and mind. Distantly, she felt him come as well, pushing himself into her and against the couch while he hovered over her and came inside her.

It took Courtney a few moments to come down from such a high. When she finally was aware of her surroundings again, Bo had finished shuddering and had slid out of her. He smoothed down her dress and then wrapped his arms around her, holding her from behind.

She closed her eyes and leaned back against him, feeling slightly wobbly and spent.

Maybe I should just give in and have an exclusive relationship, she thought, followed quickly by nipping that thought in the bud when she thought of her encounters with Raife.

She felt slightly guilty for having thought of Raife during sex with Bo, but then she wondered what it would be like to be blindfolded and tied up by Bo and *that* thought sent another little spike of lust all the way to her groin, causing her to shiver in anticipation.

"Was that...was that alright?" Bo murmured against her hair.

His tone sounded unsure and a little lost, like maybe he was afraid he'd done something wrong.

Courtney turned in his arms to face him. She went up on her tiptoes again and kissed him lightly on the lips before pulling back with a smile. "That was *very* alright."

He returned her smile, but it wavered a little as he said, "Would you stay? Just for awhile?"

She kissed him again and was surprised when she felt that stirring of need. She'd never been a more than a once a night kind of gal, but apparently that was not the case when it came to Bo Ryans.

She felt him stir against her as well. Their kiss became deeper and more demanding. Before she knew it, he'd pushed her up onto the back of the couch, but the dress still separated them. At some point, she'd kicked off her shoes.

He suddenly pulled back and gruffly asked, "Bedroom?"

Since she was busy kissing his neck and tasting the salt on his skin, she made a noise of agreement, then to her embarrassment, let out a little squeal when he picked her up and carried her to the bedroom. She decided to take the opportunity to begin unbuttoning his jacket and shirt as he stumbled through the suite.

Once in the bedroom, he placed her on the bed and pulled her dress off to toss it in a crumpled pile on the floor. She was happy to be rid of the damned piece of material since it had only gotten in the way. When that was done, she sat up and pulled down his still unzipped pants to find that, like her, he'd also gone commando to the charity event. Or maybe he just always went without underwear. Courtney filed that question away for later as he toed off his shoes, then finished removing his pants. While he was bent over, Courtney allowed her hands to rove over his naked back and butt, sending goosebumps over his skin.

He pulled off his jacket and unbuttoned his shirt the rest of the way. It took longer than Courtney would have liked, but it was also a little bit of a tease. Under the button-down shirt was a white t-shirt that he looked damn good in. He pulled that over his head as Courtney watched, thinking how much she wanted to run her hands over his six-pack abs. She had a quick moment of self-doubt when she wondered if he minded that she wasn't in perfect shape, then the thought was lost when he climbed onto the bed like a big cat contemplating its prey: Her.

Naked and shivering with anticipation, she licked her lips as he crawled toward her. He paused, drinking her in and letting her make the first move this time. Courtney took his hand and pulled him on top of her. She wrapped one leg around him, put her hands on his butt and as they kissed, she guided him inside her. As he filled her, she tipped her head back and looked into his eyes to find her own lust echoed there.

His fingers found a nipple, gently pinching it as he slid inside her again. It took him a moment to find the right angle but then he was stimulating her naturally as he slid in and out. They found a slow, steady rhythm, and he used the advantage of being on top to explore her body, squeezing her breasts and finding the exact timing with his thrust that sent jolts of electricity to her groin.

At one point, he paused while inside her and she bucked forward, trying to get more. He untangled her legs from around him and instead put them in the air, so her ankles were on his shoulders. The new position gave him more control and allowed him go even deeper inside her, causing her to cry out in surprised pleasure.

He paused. "Too much?"

She vigorously shook her head and he thrust again, while looking into her eyes.

For a moment, Courtney wasn't sure what to do with her hands now that she couldn't reach him in this new position, so he took both her hands in one of his while supporting himself with his other and pinned her hands against her stomach.

He slid into her again, and she closed her eyes as pressure began to build.

"Open your eyes," he demanded and stopped moving until she did.

A flicker of memory sparked through her. Hadn't Raife...?

She opened her eyes and found herself staring up into his eyes as he slowly pushed himself inside her. She sighed in pleasure and had to remember to keep her eyes open as that pulse of need lit up all her nerve endings.

The look in his eyes spoke of domination. That he could do what he wanted with her.

She liked it. Oh yes. She most definitely did. She wanted to show him how much, though.

She jutted her chin out and tried to give him a steely and dominating look back as she maneuvered her legs off his shoulders and back around him. Pulling her legs in, she forced him forward and further into her. He countered by pulling out and pinning her hands above her head.

"Yes," She told him, tipping her head back as he slid inside her and hit that sweet spot again. She tightened herself around him. He let out a short gasp, then his pace increased as he lost his cool control. His thrusts became harder, more demanding. In the back of her mind, she wondered what this would be like if Bo had on a mask or if she were blindfolded. The thought made her buck against him, driving him deeper. He kissed her almost possessively, taking in her moan while he thrust in just the right way to hit that sweet spot again. Then he pulled his mouth off hers just as the pressure inside her began to crest again.

She almost begged him not to stop, but suddenly he jerked on her pinned hands, a reminder that he was in charge. Then he slid himself agonizingly slowly into her while still pinning her arms overhead and looking deep into her eyes. It felt possessive and erotic as hell. For some reason, it sent Courtney over the edge. As he slid home and rocked himself against her, a wave of pure deliciousness crashed over her, and she cried out silently in pleasure as he thrust one more time, then came with her. Her mind became blissfully clear as another wave crashed over her.

His head dropped to her chest for a moment as they both fought to regain their senses.

A few minutes later, they were tucked in the bed together. Courtney had stolen his t-shirt from the floor. She now had a leg thrown over his as she lay in the crook of his arm with her head on his shoulder. He was pleasantly dozing, which was fine since Courtney was busy stressing out about their current situation and trying not to show her panic.

She wanted to just relax into his arms and fall asleep, but she had so many questions. Namely, why had he sounded just like Raife a few minutes before? Had it just been her imagination? Did she want to simplify things so badly that she just imagined him sounding like Raife? Or did Bo and Raife just have a similar turn on of having their partner look them in the eye during sex? Maybe Courtney was just reading too much into this.

Of course, the other issue was that now she didn't know where she and Bo stood. Shit. This had been her idea. Though the sex had been fantastic, had it really been a smart move? Had she just stepped into a weird relationship with Bo Ryans?

She squirmed involuntarily against him as she mentally struggled to figure out her next move.

"What?" Bo finally said in a sleepy voice.

She blew out a breath, sending a tendril of hair against Bo that tickled his skin. He opened his eyes, and she again felt that drop in her stomach and a flash of need.

How did he do that to her?

"Is this going to be the one and only time we do this or...?"

Bo shifted to prop his head on one elbow, leaving her to slide her head onto the pillow instead of his shoulder. Courtney wished he'd stayed the way they were, that way she didn't have to look directly at him. It wasn't exactly easy to remind him that she wanted to have a relaxed, nonexclusive relationship with him. Not after that mind-blowing sex.

"You still don't want to be exclusive?"

"I just," she flapped a hand in the air and then let it drop onto the covers. She tried again. "I really like you, Bo. I think dating you could be a lot of fun. But—"

"But," he said, looking a little annoyed.

"But I just got out of a relationship, and I've never really had the opportunity to...explore like this."

"Was that," he gestured to take in their recent lovemaking, "not enough?"

"It's not that," she quickly said and looked him in the eyes. Taking his face in her hands, she kissed him. "That was fantastic. Better than fantastic even," she told him with a smile when she ended the kiss.

He sighed. "But it's not enough for you to date me exclusively."

"Not right now. No. I feel like I need to learn more about myself while I have the opportunity here."

"I could help you explore," he offered in a seductive voice. His hand slid under the covers, then under her t-shirt to gently caress her breast, rubbing his thumb over her nipple before he ducked his head under the covers and pulled up the shirt, exposing her breast, to cover her nipple with his mouth.

Her breath caught in her throat at the warm, wet sensation. She was amazed that her body was still ready and responsive. How did Bo do that to her?

His hands roved further south, swirling a finger around her stomach. Teasing. His mouth left her nipple to trail down her sternum to her stomach and, reluctantly, before he could derail their conversation, she put her hands on both sides of his face and tugged him back out from under the covers.

Drawing his face towards hers, she kissed him again. Longer and deeper than before. Unfortunately, this just stirred up more longing in her own body, and when he settled his weight on her, his hard penis between her legs, rubbing against her, she realized that the kiss might have been a mistake.

When he broke the kiss, he looked her in the eyes and said, "I've never wanted anyone as much as I want you, Courtney. Not just like this but all of you. The whole package. Just to myself."

She opened her mouth, planning to protest, but he cut her off before she could speak.

"Okay."

Confused, she repeated his word. "Okay?"

"Yes. I agree to a nonexclusive relationship with you for the duration of your time at the Temple." He kissed her neck and then pulled his t-shirt over her head, once more exposing her breasts. He took her nipple in his mouth once more, sending that need through her that made her involuntarily open her legs to him. He settled in against her, moving his finger to hover just outside her, while his other hand held her hip against the bed.

She desperately wanted to push herself onto him, but he was stronger than her and wouldn't let her. She finally lifted her eyebrow up at him. "Okay...? What's the catch?"

He spoke while her nipple was still in his mouth, causing a tickling vibration that made her gasp.

"One condition," he said and slowly pushed his finger inside her.

It took Courtney a second for her brain to catch on that he'd said something. He was definitely making it difficult to concentrate. She wanted more, but his hand on her hip wouldn't let her take all of him inside her.

"What?" She finally panted looking down to find her hands in his mussed hair.

"I said, only on one condition." He let her nipple slide from his mouth and looked up at her.

"Okay" she tried not to pant. Then "Yesss," as he put a second finger inside her and moved it slowly.

He nibbled her breast, sending eddies of pleasure through her.

"You could have this all the time, Courtney." He pulled his finger out of her and moved up the bed to find her mouth with this. He drank deep and finally slid his hard penis fully inside her. She moaned, and he stopped, still filling her. She ached with need and tried to move, but the weight of his hips effectively pinned hers.

Just to show he was fully in charge, he pushed a tiny bit further into her, his body rubbing her clitoris with the movement, then pulled back that little bit, before doing it again. She grabbed his ass and tried to pull him into her once again. But he managed to stay where he was, filling her up but not moving against her in stimulation.

Somehow his being completely in charge was more of a turn on than Courtney had thought. She immediately made a mental note to up her kink level to a three with Raife.

"My terms are these..." He rocked forward that little bit and back again, making Courtney pant with desire. "Are you listening?"

"Yes!" Courtney said, wishing he'd stop talking and start moving again. She wasn't sure she could take this.

"Good." He rocked forward again, and Courtney gasped, sure she was going to go sailing over the edge soon. "I don't require you to be exclusive with me for sex as long as what you do stays here at the Temple." He was panting with need now, too. Wanting to move and feel himself inside her. She made his veins sing, and he wanted to hold her while simultaneously making her moan and gasp and pant with pleasure. Pleasure *he* gave her.

"But no dating outside of that. To the outside world, we'll

officially be dating. And I agree to the same terms, but I won't be having sex with anyone other than you."

Finally, finally, he pulled his hips back and then forward again.

"Mmm," Courtney said, not in thought but more in pleasure when he finally moved, sending that pulse through her that said her body was setting up for climax if he would just get into a damn rhythm already!

Was this what she wanted? Sex and a relationship with Bo Ryans while she had a little fun on the side with Raife and maybe some other people here at the Temple?

It seemed about as good a deal as she would get. Looking defiantly into his eyes, she tried to sound strong, which was marred by her uneven breathing as she said, "Agreed. For the duration of my stay at the Temple."

His smile was oh-so-delicious as he paired it with moving his hips to start up a real pace. "Good. Let's seal the deal." He was truly panting now, moving them more quickly to the edge.

Courtney's body had been waiting for just that. He still had her hips pinned, staying in charge of their movements. He grabbed her wrists in his hands and yanked them above her head to pin them against the bed again. She felt herself almost come just from that move of domination.

Reading that she liked him being in charge, Bo paused his movements once more. Courtney moaned in protest as he slid out and didn't fill her back up right away. Putting his weight on the hand that held her wrists, his other hand slid around her throat, first caressing then squeezing just a little. Her eyes snapped fully open, and her mouth formed an "O." Bo read the surprise in her eyes and immediately relaxed his fingers around her throat.

Maybe it had been too much?

Courtney stared up at him, realizing that she had actually liked being choked a little.

"Don't stop," she roughly told him. "Do it again, Bo."

His hand tightened again around her throat, not enough to choke her but enough to let her know she was his. He couldn't help but thrust himself inside her. Hard. Once. Twice. Then he got control of himself again before he accidently finished before her.

He wanted to make her moan. To make her crave him and no other. He wouldn't do that if he didn't make her come first.

He stopped his movements, waiting until her eyes found his again. "You're mine, now, Courtney," he said and slowly, oh so slowly, slid inside her, making sure to rub that sweet spot.

The move lit up her groin and brain, sending spasms through her that caused her to cry out. He repeated the movement, harder and faster, over and over even as she came, which somehow made her come harder. He came a second later, squeezing her throat a little harder and making her clench her muscles around his penis.

His forehead was wet with sweat when he pulled his hand from her throat and released her wrists. He had to mentally pull himself together before pulling out of her. Somehow, he felt simultaneously sated yet wanted her body even more.

He rearranged their bodies in the bed, getting behind her to make her the little spoon.

Spent and exhausted, Courtney quickly fell asleep in Bo's arms, excited about what the next few months would bring.

Long after she was asleep, Bo lay awake, feeling the rise and fall of Courtney's breathing beside him. He liked Courtney. She was beautiful, fun, and quick-witted. He liked the way she sometimes smiled wickedly while her eyes lit up with an idea.

But he worried that he'd already lost her before they'd ever really gotten a chance to start something real. He pulled her close and whispered in her ear, "I hope you'll forgive me."

But he didn't think she would once she realized that he hadn't invaded her privacy to learn about her liaisons with Raife.

He *was* Raife.

ABOUT THE AUTHOR

Penny May has always loved writing and only recently set her mind to finally giving life to the romance stories and characters who have been living rent-free in her head for years.

She also writes urban fantasy under the name J.J. Russell (but fair warning, those books are more about a snarky vampire hunter and less about sexy billionaires).

Though she grew up mostly in Tennessee, she now lives in Downeast Maine with her farmer husband and two attention-loving dogs.

Learn more about Penny May and her books by visiting:
https://www.pennymayromance.com

You can also sign up for the Penny May newsletter and get a free short story about how Bo Ryans came up with the Pleasure Temple Contest.

https://www.pennymayromance.com/newsletter

www.ingramcontent.com/pod-product-compliance
Lightning Source LLC
Chambersburg PA
CBHW070534100726
47907CB00004B/1110